NO TIME
TO SAY
Goodbye

*For all those
who have experienced the agony of
the death of a child*

NO TIME TO SAY Goodbye

PAUL ARNOTT

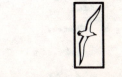

AN ALBATROSS BOOK

© Paul Arnott 1992

Published in Australia and New Zealand by
Albatross Books Pty Ltd
PO Box 320, Sutherland
NSW 2232, Australia
in the United States of America by
Albatross Books
PO Box 131, Claremont
CA 91711, USA
and in the United Kingdom by
Lion Publishing
Peter's Way, Sandy Lane West
Littlemore, Oxford OX4 5HG, England

First edition 1992

*This book is copyright. Apart from any fair
dealing for the purposes of private study,
research, criticism or review as permitted
under the Copyright Act, no part of this book
may be reproduced by any process without
the written permission of the publisher.*

National Library of Australia
Cataloguing-in-Publication data

Arnott, Paul
No time to say goodbye

ISBN 0 86760 073 X (Albatross)
ISBN 0 7459 1705 5 (Lion)

1. Children —Death — Religious aspects —
Christianity. 2. Children — Death — Psychological
aspects. 3. Parent and child. 4. Consolation.
5. Bereavement — Psychological aspects.
6. Bereavement — Religious aspects — Christianity.
I. Title

248.86

Cover illustration: Michael Mucci
Printed and bound by The Book Printer, Victoria

Contents

	Foreword	7
	Acknowledgements	9
	Introduction	11
1	First reactions	13
2	Slowing things down	28
3	Saying goodbye	40
4	Questions we ask	58
5	Reality sets in	73
6	Letting it out	88
7	Moving on	102
	Appendix I: About cot death	111
	Appendix II: Helpful resources	114

Foreword

EVERYONE WHO HAS HAD a grief experience of losing a young child should read this book because it brings into focus all that needs to be faced and worked through.

It is remarkable in its detail, all of which is necessary and meaningful. It is naked in its reality, but shot through with love and tenderness and tears. It should also be read by people who want and need to understand those who are in this situation: relatives, friends, doctors, clergy, social workers. Reading the book is a moving experience. I felt at one with those who wept for their loss.

Inevitably, the difficult questions about God's place in all this arise and Paul Arnott deals fully with these issues.

But there is a positive side. Amidst the pain, God's blessing comes from the comfort of others who bring to bear the comfort of God. Many of them have walked that way before and, in the hard reality of their own experience, have drawn on the grace of God that has given great comfort in human tragedy.

What such supporters say and share has an authenticity about it that communicates, sustaining those who are in need. What Paul has written also has that comfort and grace — and it is beautifully written! I hope it will be read by many.

Canon Jim Glennon, A.M.
*Founder of the Healing Ministry
in St Andrew's Anglican Cathedral,
Sydney, NSW*

Acknowledgements

There are so many people I want to thank for their help and support in writing this book.

Most of all, my wife Rosanne, for her advice, patience and encouragement, especially when I felt like giving up; Shirleen Wickham, our SIDS counsellor, who could not have done more; my parents Arhur and Laurel and parents-in-law Clem and Phyllis who have always been there for us; Bishop Phillip Newell, the most caring father in God anyone could ever have; Owen Salter, formerly of *On Being* magazine, for helping me take the first step; Barbara and Martin Walsh, and John and Sheryl Lockhart for sharing so freely the intimacy of their grief; John Vincent for his comments on chapter three; Archdeacon Lou Daniels, for giving me time off to write; Cynthia Fysh, for her typing in the early days; Ken Goodlet, whose editorial skills are surpassed only by his patience; Albatross Books, for conceiving the idea for this book and enabling it to come to fruition; Canon Jim Glennon, for his encouragement; Martin Gardner, for his wisdom and insight into the age-old questions of evil and suffering; those many people whose life experiences, mostly anonymous, helped bring this book to life; and last, but very certainly not least, God, without whose strength and guidance this book would never have been written.

Introduction

IT'S NOW WELL OVER FOUR YEARS since the cot death of our second child James on 17 August 1987. He was nine weeks and three days old. As in all cot deaths, the autopsy could find no reason for his death.

The English writer C. S. Lewis wrote, after the death of his wife, that no-one had told him that grief felt so much like fear. This was certainly our experience when James died. We were numb with shock, but the feeling of fear and terror were overwhelming. I vividly remember my wife Rosanne and myself lying in bed the night he died holding each other tight, trying to shut out the reality of the horror that had come into our lives.

Grief is all-encompassing. It affects the whole of our lives. In those first months there wasn't a waking moment when James wasn't in our thoughts. The reality of his death was like an everflowing stream.

One of the most devastating aspects of deaths like these are their terrible suddenness. One minute you are the parents of a beautiful healthy child and the next minute you're not. If someone has been sick or has a terminal disease, and you know they're going to die, there's at least some time to prepare yourself. But not with a sudden unexpected death.

This book was written with the bereaved parent in mind. But it can be given to anyone who has experienced the death of a loved one. If you decide to give it to a friend or relative it is probably sensible for you to have read it first. Be prepared to discuss it with them.

1
First reactions

THE MOMENT I PUT MY HAND on my son's head I knew he was dead. There is something unmistakable about the icy coldness of a dead body. I felt his hand. It, too, was cold.

James was only nine weeks old, a beautiful baby boy. But now he was dead. I screamed to my wife Rosanne to come quickly. Everything went into slow motion and I felt myself beginning to go numb. This is a nightmare, I thought. It can't be happening. I felt like a spectator watching events unfold in front of me, powerless to do anything to change what was happening.

A feeling of unreality

If you have had a child die, especially if it happened suddenly, you will know the feelings I am describing. It is a feeling of utter unreality. When I discovered the body of our son James I felt two things at once: 'This hasn't happened. This is a dream. I'll wake up soon.' I also felt: 'It's happened. My son is dead and there's nothing I can do.'

The reason it's so hard to believe it is that only a

short time before your child was alive. How could he possibly be dead?

Guilt

If your child has died, the next feeling you experience after shock will probably be guilt. You will ask yourself, 'What could I have done to prevent this?'

Gregory's grandparents found him floating face down in the swimming pool. He had been staying at his grandparents' place while his parents were away for the weekend—a second honeymoon, they said. His grandparents thought he was playing with his Duplo in the lounge. By the time they discovered he wasn't, it was too late.

Gregory's grandparents went over and over the last hour of their grandson's life in slow motion. They saw themselves eating lunch together, a memory fraught with pain and tears. They remembered their walk to the park and the Airedale puppy which almost knocked Gregory over in its excitement. And the way he had cried when they would not let him pat it because they were afraid it might bite him. They remembered setting him up with his Duplo farm to play in the lounge while they washed up the dishes from lunch.

'If only we had checked to see if the sliding door leading to the pool had been locked,' they thought. 'If only we had gone sooner to check him. If only one of us had stayed to play with him. If only we had emptied the pool last week for the winter as we had planned.'

They went over the 'if onlys' for weeks, for months.

If a child of yours has died, you will also have been down this path. It is a normal reaction. You felt responsible for that child who was totally dependent on you. Now you feel you failed them by not preventing their death.

Some people believe that it is wrong to explore the 'if onlys', but to reach a point where you are content to move beyond that soul-searching, you need to have allowed yourself to work through such thoughts and feelings.

Weeping

You may also find yourself crying and weeping over the death of your child. I say 'may', because everyone responds differently. Most people express their grief by crying. But some do not. This may be for any one of a number of reasons — they may be holding feelings in or they may be able to let their emotions out in other ways.

If you feel like crying, cry. You may be in the street or with people but, if you feel you need to cry, do it. It does not matter what people think. For most of us, tears are a gift to help wash away the pain and hurt.

Little things will trigger off your grief. A child who looks like your dead child, or what you imagine your dead child would have looked like. A song. The sound of laughter. A smell. Anything is capable of bringing it all flooding back.

Males are told from a very early age that it is weak to show their emotions — 'Only wimps cry.' We men find it hard to talk about how we feel deep down. And if we do talk about our feelings, we don't say much because we are afraid we may break down. Our biggest fear is that people will think we are weak.

The truth is that the ability to show our feelings is a sign of inner strength, but also emotional health. If you do not let your feelings of grief out in tears or in some other way, they may come out later on in physical or emotional sickness.

I spoke a while ago to a man whose daughter had died tragically in a horse-riding accident when she was only seventeen. He told me that the girl's grandfather had never expressed his grief in any visible way. Shortly after the tragedy he got Alzheimer's disease. The person I was talking to said he is convinced that his father's sickness was triggered off by his inability to let out his feelings about the death of his grand-daughter.

Tiredness and lack of concentration

One parent recalls, 'For months, every time I sat down in a comfortable chair my eyelids grew heavy and I found myself drifting off to sleep.' She told her counsellor that she was worried about always falling asleep — should she take medication to stay awake? She was advised that if she felt like sleeping, her body obviously believed that she needed to. From then on instead of fighting to stay awake, she simply went to sleep and invariably awoke feeling refreshed and better able to cope after a snooze.

Lack of concentration can also be a symptom of grief. My ability to concentrate has never been my strongest point, but following James' death I had trouble reading more than a few lines of a book at a time. How I managed to keep on producing sermons in the months following his death still amazes me.

If you find that you cannot concentrate and that you are distracted by even the slightest interruption, relax. What you are experiencing is one of the most common reactions to the death of a loved one. Linked to lack of concentration is a desire to tell the story over and over again. You may find yourself repeating the events surrounding the death of your child almost word for word. On the other hand, you may find it hard to talk about it to anyone. This is especially true of men.

Fear of losing control

Often the death of a child will create in parents a desire to try to control the world they live in. The death of your child was totally beyond your control. You felt that you were the victim, that all you could do was sit helplessly and watch events unfold before you. The fear of losing control is closely tied to two other feelings, anxiety and helplessness.

This is how the parents of a child who died in front of their eyes in a car accident described it: 'We felt so helpless. We could see it all happening, like it was in slow motion. But there was nothing we could do to stop it. It all happened too fast.'

The feeling of frustration created by that helplessness may cause parents to become over-cautious and over-protective. Cot death parents may become paranoid about the slightest cough or snuffle in their remaining children.

If you are the parent of a child who drowned, you may become paranoid about letting any of your other children near water, or even out of your sight. People will encourage you not to worry and tell you that your children will be all right in the care of others, but you feel you know differently because you have had a child die. You have been sensitised to the possibility of a child of yours dying. Before your child died you knew it was a possibility. Now you know that it happens because it happened to you. And it could happen again.

Swinging in and out of reality

All death has a suddenness to it. Even when a loved one has been ill for months or years there is a feeling of suddenness about the final death. But when a child dies without warning, the suddenness is terrible.

How does that suddenness affect us?

When your child dies in an accident you have had no time to prepare for that death. One moment you have a live child, the next a dead body. When there is time to prepare for death, people are able to adjust more at their own pace, but sudden death forces that adjustment to be done much more quickly. You will find yourself swinging in and out of reality. One moment you may feel overwhelmed by the reality of what has happened; the next you may feel it is nothing but a nightmare from which you soon hope to awaken.

Many bereaved parents say they sit around waiting for something to happen — anything that will change the reality of what has taken place. Rosanne and I half-expected someone to knock on our front door with our son in their arms and the news that it had all been some sort of sick joke. Of course we didn't really believe that would happen, but we desperately hoped it would.

You may find yourself experiencing all kinds of bizarre fantasies. What is happening is that your mind is struggling to take it in. One parent told me that after her child died, she kept having the thought: 'She's not really dead. If I look hard enough and search far enough I'll find her.' She said that she knew that this was untrue, but she half-believed it.

Fear of going crazy

It is not unusual for people to feel that they are going out of their minds. When our child died, there were times in the first few months when both of us felt that we could go insane. It was as if we were standing on the edge of the cliff of sanity and one little push could have had us over that edge. For us what prevented our going over was our faith in God. What is important is to realise it is normal to feel this way.

The fear of going crazy may also make it difficult for you to get to sleep, or you may find yourself wide awake at 3.00 a.m. for no obvious reason. Sleep difficulties are very common. So, too, are dreams and nightmares.

Dreams are often the way we work through unresolved conflict in our waking lives. The death of a child is a massive unresolved conflict, so don't be surprised if you dream a lot. If you remember your dreams, write them down. Keep a pen and pad by the bed. You may find them revealing.

Anger, resentment and blame

When our son James died, I didn't feel angry at first. I think there was too much else going on for me to have time to. But two months later I found myself becoming angry at everything. I was angry at other parents who had healthy babies. I was angry at some parents who didn't seem to care enough for their children. I was angry at the injustice and unfairness of healthy children dying when they were so greatly loved. I was angry at the sun for daring to shine. I was angry at everything and everyone. I was angry at God.

I remember being so angry one day that I hit a solid pine dining room door in the house we lived in. The door was very thick and it was a very painful experience, although I did retain enough self-control to avoid hitting it full on with a clenched fist. I knew that would break my hand and I wanted to hurt the door more than myself.

Anger will express itself in a great variety of ways. You may not realise at first, as I didn't, where the anger is coming from. You may become angry over the most trivial things.

Resentment and bitterness may be anger that you haven't expressed. When we push down feelings of anger they can pop up months or even years later. These feelings of undealt-with anger can be very destructive.

You may feel bitter towards your partner whom you hold responsible for what happened. Instead of talking openly about your anger you may have held the feelings in. You may even feel bitter towards the child who died. 'How dare you die and leave me!' We don't expect our children to die before us. When they do it seems so unfair, so wrong. When a child dies we look for a reason and we look for someone to hold responsible.

Almost all of us hold God responsible — more on this later — but often the person who is easier to get at is our partner. This is why such strain can be put on a relationship after a child dies. If there are problems already, it usually makes them worse, unless you are able to get it out into the open and talk about it. Or seek professional counselling. Even strong relationships may break down if people begin to blame one another. It is very important to talk to each other about how you are feeling.

The parents of Gregory, with whose story we began, had a very good relationship. But his death almost drove them apart. It was the first time they had ever left him overnight with anyone. His father felt relaxed about leaving him. His mother did not. She was worried the entire weekend.

When the phone call came, she half-expected it. She felt that if her husband hadn't convinced her to leave Gregory he would still have been alive. His father felt tremendous guilt because he also believed he was responsible for his son's death. It was only their eventual decision to seek professional counselling which prevented divorce.

Isolation from others

Fear of leaving the house and seeing people can be another reaction to the death of a child. When our son died, my wife Rosanne felt that everyone in the small country town we lived in must have known.

'There she is, the poor thing,' she almost heard them saying. This can be very hard to cope with. Sometimes, though, we may feel the opposite. 'How can they just go on living their everyday lives as if nothing has happened? Don't they care that our child is dead?' We may also be struck by the triviality of daily life. So much of what we do may seem unimportant. All of this can give us a sense of alienation from others.

We can find that it is possible to have a house full of mourners and feel desperately lonely. This is because of the unique nature of grief. No-one else can grieve for us, not even our partner. It is a journey that we make alone. Others can share in it, but they cannot travel the same road. This is a shock to many couples.

Terry and Janet were as close as any couple could be. In their eleven years of married life they had done everything together. But when their three-year-old daughter Chrissy was killed by a hit-and-run driver, they suddenly discovered they could not grieve together. This was a real tension for them because they had always shared everything else.

With the help of grief counselling, they came to see that women and men often grieve differently. Women are much more likely to have their self-image changed by the death of a child. When your child dies, your whole world is shattered. Once your days were busy and full: now there seems very little to do, especially if it was your only child who died.

But the self-image of a man, should he be the one

working outside the home, is often shaped far more by his work and he still has that. Most men throw themselves back into their jobs very quickly after the death of a child as a way of coping. But all of this can give each partner a sense of isolation from the other.

Feelings of failure and disappointment

Often the death of your child can make you feel you have failed as a parent. In our society, success as parents is measured, wrongly I believe, not only in the performance of our children, but also in whether or not they are alive.

This attitude is reflected in this comment, made to a mother who had one twin die: 'Oh well, at least you've still got Katherine.' The unspoken message can be that you failed with your child who died, but you still have the chance to succeed with the one who is alive. Some people will say quite thoughtless things, because they have no idea of the view from the inside.

Another powerful reaction to the death of a child can be disappointment. When a child is born, there are born with it a huge number of expectations, many of them unspoken. You may have hoped that your child would follow in your footsteps as a chess player, football player, or in some other way. You may have been looking forward to the first step or the first day at school or teaching your child to cook or swim or to learn to drive. Some months after James died, I realised that one of my unspoken hopes was to teach him to play cricket. It hurt so much to know I never would.

Sadness and depression

Feeling sad is a normal and healthy response to the death of your child. But there is pressure on many of us not to feel sad or at least not to stay sad for too long.

Three weeks after the funeral of her child, Julie received a note from the minister who took the service saying, 'I hope you are back on top of things by now.' He had obviously never had a child die and possessed few skills in grief counselling.

There is a number of reasons that people want us to get over our sadness quickly. The first is that often our sadness makes them feel sad and many people don't cope with this, because they feel it is wrong to be sad. For them the aim of human existence is to be happy all the time.

Another reason is that our grief may have triggered off undealt-with griefs in their lives and they would rather push them down than deal with them.

The other obvious reason that those outside our immediate family recover more quickly is that our child meant less to them than to us so the pain and grief are also less.

Some people feel that it is okay to feel sad, but not all right to become depressed. Depression, they argue, is sadness or anger that has been repressed and is therefore unhealthy. But grieving is grieving and because we are all different, anything goes. You may feel depressed by the death of your child, but this is not necessarily unhealthy. It only becomes wrong if you become stuck in your grief by denying that the death has happened.

If Gregory's drowning had become for his

grandparents an endless nightmare in which they wallowed for years, this would probably indicate that they were refusing to accept its reality.

It is important to accept our feelings, to embrace them and fully explore them. But having done that, we must choose to move on and in the end this is a choice. We can choose to move on into life or to stay on the merry-go-round of grief. We explore this more fully later.

The uniqueness of grief

Everyone responds to death in a different way and every death is as unique as every life. You may have experienced most of the things I have described so far in the pages of this book. You may have experienced very few of them. Your experiences may be quite unusual.

For some, for example, there can be unexpected physical symptoms. When our son James died, my wife Rosanne felt a pain in the middle of her chest for months afterwards. At first she thought she might be having a heart attack but, as the pain came and went, she realised it was a physical manifestation of her grief.

These individual responses don't mean you are strange. They simply mean that you respond in your own unique way. Your personality will influence the way you grieve. Grief has been described as the price we pay for loving and attachment. But the ways we experience it are very different. Grief and pain are intensely personal. Respond in the way you want, not the way you feel others want you to.

I have noticed that often when people rush to someone who is crying because of the death of a loved one they are really comforting themselves. By touching, they can be saying, 'Please don't cry. You're upsetting me so much you are making me feel like crying, too, but I'm too scared to let it out.' We must do what we feel is right for us. We must go with our feelings, not our intellects.

* * *

A word to carers

The greatest gift you can give a bereaved parent is your presence. Words are not very important. Often we feel we need to apologise for having come or try to find a reason for the death. We don't. The best thing we can do is just be there.

When our son died, the person who helped me most was a fellow clergyman whose own father had died only two weeks before. He came to our house with tears in his eyes, but no words. He was too upset to say anything, but knowing he had just experienced the death of his father helped me a great deal. He knew what it was like from the inside.

It is also very important to use the name of the dead child. The temptation is to avoid the child's name because we're worried we'll upset the parents. But this can be very hurtful to bereaved parents. They haven't forgotten the name. If you avoid using it, it can make them feel that you are trying to pretend the child never existed.

It is important to allow parents to talk about the child if they want to. A parent may want to go over and over the story of their child's death. This will probably be both upsetting and irritating to the people listening, but it is crucial that they be allowed to do it. Repetition is part of coming to terms with the reality of death.

Also try to avoid using euphemisms. For instance, instead of talking about the loss of their child, talk about the death of their child. This may sound a harsh thing to say, but it is the reality. As Janet Deveson Lord, author of *When a Baby Suddenly Dies*, once pointed out to me, to talk about the loss of a baby or a child implies that the child may be found again.

Whatever we may believe about the life to come, when a child has died they are lost to us forever in this world. No matter how harsh this may seem it is reality. So we are far better off expressing that reality in our words by saying they are dead, not lost. The more fully a parent is able to face reality, the sooner he or she can continue the journey of grief.

The other important thing we can do for the grieving parent is to be available to do practical jobs for them. When we are in deep shock even making a cup of tea can seem like an insurmountable task.

The morning after James died, a good friend of ours offered to spend the whole day answering our phone and taking messages. When James died, some very close friends of ours dropped everything to be with us. Just having them there was a great comfort.

2
Slowing things down

THERE IS A TERRIBLE SUDDENNESS to the unexpected death of a child. Most of us expect to die before any of our children, so when a child of ours dies it's a tremendous shock. This is especially true of the death of a baby.

If someone we love has been sick or has had a terminal disease, there is some time to prepare for their eventual death. This is why families of people who die after a long illness often appear to cope so well. They have done most of their grieving already.

But when our child dies suddenly, there is no time to prepare ourself for their death. There is no time to say goodbye. One moment we are the parent of a living child; the next moment we are not. It's that brutal. However, there are a number of ways to slow down events after our child has died.

Touching our child
It is only in recent years that we have become aware of how important it is for parents to hold and touch the body of a dead child. Until recently, most

bereaved people in the Western world were discouraged, sometimes strongly, from touching their dead children. Sometimes family or medical staff have suggested they not even see their child's body.

We have a friend whose first child died ten years ago in a cot death, but she never saw her daughter's body. It was common practice in maternity wards for the body of a stillborn baby to be quickly covered with a sheet and whisked away before the mother had a chance to look at her baby.

Now the parents of stillborn babies are encouraged to hold and cuddle their children for as long as they like. Often they are encouraged to name them and have them photographed. Parents who took photos will tell you how wonderful it is to have that concrete memory of their dead child. Many parents have also taken hand and footprints of their dead child or a lock of hair.

This is one mother's description of what happened after the birth of her stillborn son, Benjamin:

> His little face wore a sad expression. His head was very soft and his skin had started to blister. I kept saying, 'Isn't that sad. The poor little thing.' But inside me I felt nothing at all, just an empty numb feeling.
>
> A friend took photos of him and then he was wrapped up and [my husband Martin] held him as I wasn't yet ready. It was a sad picture, my dear husband holding his baby son. He stood there looking down at Benjamin and he seemed so vulnerable.
>
> While [my friend Helen] and Martin held him, I hugged them and I gradually prepared myself to hold him. Next Helen bathed him. She talked to him in a soft gentle voice and I was so glad she did

what I was unable to do. Benjamin was dried and dressed. Then they took his footprints and handprint and I held him.

We were left alone for a while and then were moved to another room where we were able to spend the rest of the night, just the three of us. One of the sisters moved his bed directly under a light, but I asked a nurse to move him back out of the glare. I wanted to have him near me, but I couldn't look at his little face all the time.

Now we look back and wish we had put him between us and held him close. There's so much we'd have done differently. But at the time it's all so new and fast and strange and scary. After I got dressed, I sat in the armchair with my baby in my arms. I rocked and cried for all I had lost. I wanted him so badly. I loved him so much and the pain of the grief was unbearable.

Then Mum came. I was unsure of how she would react. She took her tiny little grandson and wept. I asked her if she'd like to see his perfect little body. He was so beautiful — such a perfectly formed little man, with a high forehead just like his Daddy's. I felt detached and unable to grasp the full reality of it all. It was as though I was watching myself go through the whole experience.

I remember showing his photos to a nurse. Tears rolled down her cheeks.

Helen told me we could stay with Benjamin as long as we liked, but we felt it was time to go. The hardest thing was leaving the hospital without our long-awaited baby.

The year before our son died, we had seen a film in Melbourne about the importance of parents holding their stillborn babies. After the death, we knew instinctively that for us it was the right thing to do.

I say 'for us', because it is so individual. It feels right to most parents to hold and cuddle their dead children. But there may be some parents who don't feel right about doing that. You have to do what feels right for you at the time. What is important is that you realise you are able to hold your child if you want to.

After we had called the doctor and ambulance and they had not been able to resuscitate him, we held and cuddled James and said goodbye. Our eldest child Alice also cuddled him and kissed him goodbye. She was only three at the time, so she didn't fully understand what had happened to her brother. She was more worried about Mummy and Daddy who wouldn't stop crying.

Many parents to whom I have spoken after the death of their children believed at the time that they were not allowed to touch the body of their child. One father told me he had once been told that a dead body automatically became the property of the State. So when their daughter died, he and his wife felt they should not touch her until after the police had come.

I don't know where this belief came from, but in my experience it is widespread. And it is totally untrue. There is no law or government regulation which prevents parents from touching the body of their dead child. It may be that the police would prefer the body not be touched until they arrive, but there is no law which forbids it.

Keeping our child at home

Keeping our dead child at home for a while can help slow things down. There is no law which says we have to let the undertaker remove the body of our dead child before we are ready to let them.

This is still a very real regret of mine. After we had cuddled James and held him, I went to ring my parents to tell them their only grandson was dead, the hardest phone call I have ever had to make in my life. (The death of a grandchild is a double grief for grandparents, for they grieve not only over the death of their grandchild, but also for their child.) The undertaker had arrived and asked my wife to dress James in whatever clothes she wanted. Then she handed him over and he took him away.

Rosanne tells me she didn't realise the undertaker was going to take James and I certainly didn't expect him to be gone when I came back from the phone.

I still feel I hadn't properly said goodbye to him. If we had our time over again, we would keep him at home for longer. That was our right, though we didn't realise it then. That is the right of every parent of a dead child. You don't have to hand over the body of your child until you are ready to.

As long as the child didn't die of an infectious disease, which would make the body a public health risk, we are legally allowed to keep the child at home. In Australia, the period we can keep them varies from State to State. Victoria has a law requiring that a funeral be conducted within seven days, unless it takes longer because someone is flying home from overseas. You would need to check with your State health department to be sure.

In one particular case, we know of parents who decided to keep their child's body at home overnight until the funeral. I don't think we would have kept James' body in the house overnight, even if we had realised we were able to. But this is where grief is so personal. You have to do what helps you. Keeping your child's body may help to slow down the suddenness of his or her death. It may be very positive or it may not. Only you can decide.

The people who kept their son's body at home until the funeral dressed him in his pyjamas and laid him on his bed. Members of the family would spend time with him, in quietness, talking to him, weeping, praying, just being with him. His younger brother even once pulled up his pyjama top to show a friend the marks on his chest from the accident in which he died.

You may find the thought of having your dead child at home very helpful or you may not. What is important is knowing what you are legally allowed to do and doing what is helpful for you.

Obviously what is helpful for you may not be helpful for other family members, so you need to discuss it and arrive at a joint decision. You may have to push hard to make this conversation take place, because often other family members won't want to talk, especially about such emotional matters. But it will be worth it. When change is in the air, the more communication that can take place the better.

Carlene and Peter's fourteen-year-old-son Raymond died of a massive asthma attack on a ferry in the middle of Sydney Harbour. It happened so suddenly and was so severe that there was no time to get medical help. Even if there had been a doctor on board the ferry, Raymond would probably still have died.

Peter and Carlene lived with Peter's parents in an inner suburb of Sydney. They both wanted to keep Raymond at home until the day of the funeral and realised it was their right to do so. But Peter's parents were horrified at the thought of their dead grandson lying in a coffin in their lounge room.

At first they refused even to discuss the issue and, when they finally agreed to talk, it developed into a shouting match. It was only when Carlene broke down and wept that Peter's parents realised how much it meant to their children to have Raymond's body at home. Despite their feelings of revulsion they agreed.

Raymond's body lay in the lounge for three-and-a-half days until the afternoon of the funeral. His grandparents lay awake the entire first night thinking of the body of their much-loved grandson lying cold and still in the room in which they had so often sat as a family.

His parents, on the other hand, were tremendously comforted by the knowledge that their son's body was lying nearby in familiar surroundings, rather than in the cold sterility of a funeral parlour. They visited their son a number of times during the night to talk to him or simply to sit with him. The idea of sitting with a dead body may seem strange to some people, yet we will spend days sitting with a loved one who is dying. That they are dead doesn't change the fact that the body belonged to someone we loved.

Before our son died, I used to say I didn't care what people did with my body after I died because I wouldn't be there. To me a body was just an empty shell, of little importance once the spirit had gone.

But James' death changed my feelings totally. Here was the body of someone I loved as much as I loved my wife or my daughter or myself. Even though he had left his body, it was still precious because it was the body of my son. It was the body of a baby my wife had carried in her own body. It was the body of a son I held with such pride and joy moments after his birth.

Dressing our child

Many parents find that dressing their dead child helps them slow things down. Also it is something concrete they can do for the child. One of the deepest longings we have when our child dies is to hold them in our arms, to cuddle them, to hug them. We want to do as much as we can for them materially.

Choosing clothes for them to wear when they were alive was part of being a parent. Choosing clothes for them to wear when they are dead is also. It helps us, in a small way, to take control of the situation. When our child dies, we feel that we have no control over what has happened. We feel events have been taken out of our hands. Anything we can do to help us feel we have regained control of some of these events can only be positive.

So thoughtfully choose clothes for your child to wear, perhaps their favourite clothes. You may even wish to sew special clothes for your child to wear, especially in the case of a pre-term stillborn baby where clothes of the appropriate size are not available.

Few undertakers will object to your choosing clothes for your child to be dressed in, but some may not be open to the idea of your dressing them. It is your right to dress your child if you want to and most funeral directors will oblige. But there may be some who object because they feel it is their role, not yours, or they may be concerned for you.

If a post-mortem has been carried out on your child's body, there is a possibility of seepage of blood from the incisions on the head and torso. Some undertakers will discourage parents from dressing their child because they are concerned about the effect on the parents.

Also in the case of a stillborn child when it has been dead for several days the undertaker may need to dress the baby because the tiny body is very fragile. While the undertaker's concern for the parents may be justified, what's important is that parents know they can dress their child if they want to.

Often parents place in the coffin things which belonged to the child like cuddly toys, books, flowers, letters or even a photo. While we know such things will be of no use to them, it's often a great comfort to us as parents. You may also like to take a photo of your child in the coffin.

Exercising our autopsy rights

An autopsy or post-mortem is conducted on the body of anyone whose cause of death cannot be verified by a doctor. It is almost always conducted when someone dies suddenly. A pathologist examines the internal organs in an attempt to identify the cause of death. The pathologist then writes a report on his findings which goes to the coroner who conducts a public inquest into the death of your child.

Some coroners may be less than willing to provide a copy, either because they don't realise it's our right or they may be concerned about the effect the graphic descriptions of an autopsy report may have on us. But as we have the right to attend the inquest and could, if we wanted, take notes, it makes little sense for a coroner to deny any parent a copy of the report.

If you decide you would like a copy, find out who the coroner was by ringing the local police station and write to him explaining why you would like it. When you receive a copy of the autopsy, it might be best to take it, unopened, to your GP and ask him to help translate it for you. The report is written in medical terminology, which can be confusing. It's better to have your doctor on hand to help explain it than to read it alone and risk coming to a wrong conclusion about your child's death.

I still remember the visit of two nervous-looking policemen to our house on a cold Tasmanian October evening. They had a copy of the report, which we had requested from the coroner some weeks earlier, and they wanted to make sure we knew what graphic details we would encounter when we read it.

I'm sure their motive was concern for us, but their question, 'Why do you want a copy of it?', felt like an interrogation. It was none of their business to know why we wanted a copy of it. The coroner had decided to make a copy available to us. Their job was simply to deliver it. This incident highlights a common problem.

Medical staff, police and even coroners are given little if any training in how to deal with bereaved families. They are trained to diagnose disease, catch criminals and conduct inquests, but not to deal with people in grief. This is not their fault. It's the fault of the system that trains them.

Those responsible for training these professionals need to do more than pay lip service to the importance of providing them with skills in handling bereaved people. So much harm can be avoided by a few basic skills which are quickly acquired. Knowing what to say and what not to say is crucial for any professional handling people in grief. You don't have to become a grief counsellor to deal effectively with a person in shock.

Viewing the body

I usually encourage bereaved parents to view the body of their dead child, especially if they were not there when the child died. This helps parents to accept the reality of what has happened.

The father of a friend of mine died while she was in the United States. When she arrived home, the only way she could accept he was dead was to go and see his body in the funeral parlour. If we don't see the body of our child there is a danger we will have real problems believing they are dead.

This can happen to the family of someone who is drowned and whose body is never found. Family members can have enormous problems accepting their loved one is dead. The same is true of those terrible cases of children disappearing, never to be seen again. You never quite believe they are dead.

While you must do what you feel is right, you need to be sure your decision not to see your child's body will not be something you always regret. It is a very personal decision.

My father chose not to see his mother after she died, although he was invited to. His reason was that he wanted to remember her the way she was, alive and well. It is a decision he has never regretted and we must respect such decisions, rather than try to force people into doing what we believe is best for them. People need to be given the options, without bias or pressure, and allowed to choose for themselves. Of course that's easier said than done, especially when some strong-minded individual is convinced they know what's best for the whole family.

If you do decide to see your child's body, take your time, even if the undertaker seems busy. You should expect your child to look pale and feel cold to touch. If you have anything you want to say to them, tell them, or if there's something you regret having said or done, tell them that, too. It is a time for getting things out in the open, for being honest. It's a time for making sure there are no regrets, for tying up any loose ends.

3
Saying goodbye

THE FUNERAL IS ONE OF THE MOST important parts of the grieving process. It gives us the opportunity to say goodbye to our children and to pay tribute to them. Paying tribute is enormously important. It is the main reason I write this book. After James died, I discovered within myself a burning desire to make his life count.

The funeral brings home the reality of the death of the person we love. It is painful, but it is helpful, because it provides an ending to a life. It is a clearly marked cut-off point. Even the families of people whose bodies have never been found after an accident need some kind of memorial service to help them start to come to terms with what has happened.

The time of the funeral

The first decision to be made is when the funeral should take place. The funeral director and the minister, if you call one in, will give you whatever help you need. Remember the professionals involved are there to help you, especially the funeral director whom you are hiring. So don't be afraid to tell them what you want. If what you ask for is not possible or is inappropriate, they will soon tell you.

The funeral is usually held within two or three days, but in the case of a sudden unexpected death, especially that of a child, experience has taught us it is wise to add a day. This helps slow down the suddenness. It gives more time to take in all that has happened, which means we will cope better in the long run.

When our child dies suddenly the temptation can be to 'get it over and done with' as quickly as possible because it is so painful. Our son James died on a Monday. We could have had his funeral on the Wednesday, but the advice we received was to delay it until the Thursday. We are very glad we did, because it gave us more time.

We've since spoken to a number of parents who held the funeral service very quickly after the death of their child. In one case the funeral was held the next day. Almost all these parents later regretted having had the funeral so quickly. We need that extra time to begin to come to terms with the immensity of what has happened to us. I often feel that our son's death was like an enormous bomb being exploded in the very heart of our family, the reverberation of which we are still feeling.

The kind of funeral

Having decided when the funeral will be, you now need to decide what kind of service you would like. Once again the funeral director and minister, if you have one, will help you. You may be so much in shock that all you want to do is to hand over these arrangements to someone else. If that is how you are feeling, that's fine. But if you are able to help plan the funeral, it will make it more meaningful for you and give you more of a feeling of control over what is happening to you and around you.

First, you need to decide where the funeral will be and who will conduct it. Most people still have a service in a church or funeral chapel. But it is also possible for it to be held in a home or a garden. If the funeral is held in a public place, permission must be obtained from the local authorities.

The funeral can be conducted by anyone, because it is not a legal procedure like a wedding. But if it is held in a church, it can only be conducted by someone authorised by that church.

Where you want the funeral to be held and who you want to take it will obviously be determined by how religious you are. Whether you have a minister or a civil celebrant conduct the funeral, it is important that you have confidence in them. Many funeral parlours offer the services of a member of their staff who is an experienced civil celebrant.

Sometimes when a child dies it is decided to hold a private funeral. This is almost always accompanied by a decision to request no condolences, no cards, flowers or expressions of sympathy. Once again you need to do what feels right for you. But if you decide to have a private funeral, you need to be sure you have thought through all the implications.

A private funeral will mean none of your friends will be able to come unless you decide to invite some very close friends. It will mean, too, that you will cut yourself off from people who want the opportunity of expressing their love for you and your dead child by attending the funeral. Sometimes the unspoken message of a private funeral can be 'please stay away'! If a friend hasn't been to the funeral, often they will not know what to say the next time they see you.

Often, too, people who want a private funeral will also opt for only a graveside service. The danger is that the service will be so brief that it won't succeed in achieving the purpose of a funeral, to provide a ritual to enable the bereaved to begin to accept the reality of the death of their loved one.

In the end, though, having considered the options, you may still choose to have a private funeral. In my experience most people who decide on a private funeral do so because they just can't cope with sharing their grief with anyone except the immediate family.

The next decision you have to make is whether you want your child's body to be buried or cremated. It is likely that you will have a strong view one way or the other. Most people seem to. We decided to have James buried because neither of us likes the idea of cremation, for no particular reason. We just don't like it. To have him buried seemed more natural. But I have spoken to some people who feel cremation is much better than burial.

I heard recently of a man who had his wife's body cremated and took her ashes to her favourite beach. Apparently she walked on the beach every morning and loved it. He opened the lid of the box containing her ashes and gently poured them onto the sand. The next wave washed over them and they were gone. He said there was such a feeling of rightness about what he had done.

Burial at home?

It is both legal and possible in Australia for the body to be buried somewhere in the grounds of your home. However, there are a number of conditions which vary from State to State, so if you decided to explore this option you would need to contact your local council and State health department. The grave must be dug to a certain depth, must be a certain distance from the house and you must guarantee you will be living in that home for a certain number of years.

John and Sheryl Lockhart —of whom we hear more in chapter 6 — chose to have their son buried in their backyard. They said it was quite a struggle to find out exactly what the requirements were, but they got there in the end.

It is perhaps worth warning you that if you decide to do anything unconventional in regard to the funeral or burial of your child you may encounter some opposition. Sometimes public officials find it easier to say, 'No, you can't do that,' rather than to find out whether you can.

If you happen to be the first person ever to ask the local council about home burial the 'No, you can't' may really mean, 'No-one has ever asked that one before and I don't much like the sound of it'! You may need to be persistent to get what you want — and ask for the person in charge, not the clerk at the front desk.

It is also possible for you to make your own coffin, but again you would need to check the local regulations. Some parents have made special clothes for their children to be buried or cremated in. The mother of Benjamin found making clothes for her still-born son a very meaningful experience:

> I was able to make Benjamin's coffin clothes and I'm so glad because it meant so much to be able to use a favourite blouse to make into a tiny bonnet and gown for him. Although it was sad, it was special to be able to make something for him that he could actually wear. I had already been deprived of the pleasures of knitting and sewing for him when he was alive.
>
> Mum and I sewed them together and as we stitched we cried and thought and talked about our little Benjamin. The tiny blue rosebuds Mum embroidered on the bonnet were exquisite. [My husband Martin] bought Benjamin a tiny little white teddy and I wrote him a letter telling him all about our family and how much we loved him and missed him.

Helping children cope

Many parents ask me whether I think they ought to take their other children to the funeral. I always tell them the same thing: 'Ask them if they want to go and let them decide.' Obviously very young children might not know whether they want to go or even what it's all about. But as a general rule of thumb, let them make up their own minds. Most children I know will tell you very smartly whether they want to be there or not.

We took our eldest daughter Alice to her

brother's service in the church but not to the graveside, which now as we look back was probably a mistake. Alice was only three when James died and we felt the graveside service would mean nothing to her. It wasn't until months afterwards when she began to ask questions about where James was that we realised we should have had her there.

Three-year-olds are very concrete thinkers and being told their little brother is in heaven with Jesus means nothing to them. They want to know where his body is and, because Alice hadn't gone to the graveside, she hadn't seen the casket with his body in it go into the ground. Even though she wouldn't have understood, at least she would have had the memory there for us to build on later.

Almost two years after James' death, we found Alice outside the front of the church trying to prise off the wall one of the metal plaques behind which people's ashes were kept. The plaques were firmly cemented in and she had no success, but it drove home again the fact that she still hadn't grasped what had happened to her baby brother's body.

The first thing we need to realise about children and death is that children grieve differently from adults. They also grieve according to their age and stage of understanding. If we had realised this then we would have done some things very differently.

Although one child differs from another in the way he expresses his grief, some age group generalisations can provide helpful guidelines.

❏ *One- to three-year-olds*
Children in this age group react to the death of

someone they love mainly at a feelings level. They quickly pick up the emotional atmosphere around them. They can feel loss and the emotions that follow, but they don't realise that death is forever. The death of a brother or sister will almost certainly be their first experience of losing someone they love. This isn't to say that children of this age can't feel very deeply, but they seem to bounce back more quickly than most adults.

When children this age begin to ask questions, it is best to respond to the feeling behind the question, rather than trying to explain what happened or where the dead child is. For example, if a younger child asks when he can go and visit the dead child, it is better to pick up on the fact that they may be missing them. You might say, 'Are you feeling sad that John isn't here to play with you right now?' If your guess was wrong, their reply will soon tell you. Young children don't think abstractly, so avoid using abstract pictures.

After James died, we were trying to explain to Alice that he hadn't felt any pain so we said it was just like going to sleep. As soon as we'd spoken the words, we realised how Alice could have misunderstood. If she thought that dying was just like going to sleep, we could have very easily had a little girl who didn't want to go to sleep for fear of dying. Fortunately, we quickly corrected our initial blunder without doing our daughter any permanent harm.

It is most important with children of this age to include them in the family's grief. Let them be part of what's happening. They also need a great deal of reassurance, both verbal and physical — lots of hugs and touching.

❑ *Four- to seven-year-olds*
Children this age will have had some experience of death. They will have seen plants or pets or fictional characters on TV die. We can build on these experiences and use them to help our other children better understand what has happened.

Only a year before James died, while we were attending a wedding in Melbourne, Alice and an older friend had found a dead bird in a garden. The friend had talked very sensitively to Alice about what had happened to the bird and they had buried it together. This experience obviously had a great impact on Alice, because four months later when we were back in Melbourne and walked past the same garden where the bird was buried, she wanted to look for it to see if it was still there. We were able to use the experience to help explain that James had stopped breathing just like the bird had and had been buried.

Children this age tend to think of death as being temporary. When they shoot someone in a game, the person always gets up again. They don't stay dead. They may respond to the news of the death of a brother or sister in a very matter-of-fact way because they don't realise it is permanent. When James died, though Alice cuddled him and said goodbye, she was more involved playing with her older friend Joy.

These children are often very interested in the physical and biological aspects of death, so the death should be explained to them in these terms. Children in this age group are still concrete thinkers. The day after James died, Alice demonstrated to us exactly what James looked like when we found him, floppy and loose. This did nothing for us, but was obviously helpful to her.

Another trait of children this age is their ability to ask a very deep question about life or death and then move on very quickly. Five-year-old Sarah, a week after the drowning of her baby brother Justin in a backyard pool, suddenly announced, 'I wonder if Justin is allowed to swim in heaven, Mummy? It may not be as dangerous to swim there as it is down here.' And then in the next breath she went on to say, 'What's for tea tonight, Mummy? I'd really like fish and chips.'

Now as we look back, we can see we should have dealt more with the physical aspects of death which Alice could understand than with the spiritual side which she couldn't really grasp. Instead of telling her that James had gone to heaven to be with Jesus, we should have explained that James' body was dead because he stopped breathing and that his body would be buried. It is enough at this age to reassure them that the dead child is 'safe with God'.

It is also very important only to answer the question being asked. If we are asked where the dead child has gone, it is enough to say their body is in the ground and their spirit is with God. We don't need to give them a complicated explanation about where heaven is and what it's like unless they are asking. If you are not sure whether you believe in the existence of heaven or of God or if you are quite sure you don't, you need to decide whether you want to share your doubts with your children.

At this stage the most important thing is to help them understand what death is. My wife Rosanne remembers some six months after James died how Alice asked her out of the blue, 'Mummy, how did Daddy know James was dead?' For the next few months, Alice often told us or other people 'James is dead' with the emphasis on the word 'dead' as if she were beginning to understand what it meant.

Another example of the concrete thinking of this age group was Alice's comments about heaven. She announced one day that she would like to go and 'visit James in heaven'! When Rosanne said we couldn't just go and visit James whenever we like because we didn't go to heaven until we died, she said, 'Is he busy?' To children this age, heaven is a geographical place which they can visit any time they want.

In the end we suggested to Alice that she write a letter to James, saying whatever she wanted to tell him. Of course as soon as she'd finished, she wanted to post it which was yet another challenge. We explained we couldn't send letters to heaven, but that we were sure God knew what was in her letter and that we could ask him to tell James what she'd said in it. So that is what we did. She was happy and we had learned something new.

There is also a danger that remaining siblings might misinterpret the dead child's death. Sometimes a child might blame the dead child for leaving them, particularly if they are the only child left.

They might even blame themselves. 'I was naughty' or 'I was so horrible to my sister that she died'. This is not uncommon. We feel guilt as parents; why shouldn't children also feel it?

It is also not unusual for children having a fight to either say or think, 'I wish you were dead.' There is often a love/hate relationship with a new baby, which sensibly dealt with will cause no problems, unless the baby happens to die, in which case the other child may feel they have brought about the death.

If there are such times as this when you get out of your depth and need to call in professional counselling help, this doesn't mean you've failed as a parent. We all need professional help sometimes as parents and these days there is more help available than ever before. There are trained grief counsellors and family mediation centres which can be used if necessary. A list of these is in *Appendix II*.

Another common problem with children in this age group is sleep disturbance after the death of a sibling. For the first few nights after James' death, Alice wouldn't even go to sleep unless she was in her sleeping bag on the lounge room floor while we sat and talked. She needed to be right with us. At first we thought it was because she was afraid of dying herself — 'If it can happen to my brother it can happen to me, too.'

But we soon realised her real fear was not that she would die herself, but that either one or both of us might die and she would be left alone. I can't remember what it was that alerted us to what was going on but, as soon as we realised, it all made sense. Alice slept in the lounge for about four nights, then moved into our room at the foot of our bed for several weeks and finally back into her own room. But she continued to have disturbed sleep.

About a year after James died, she began to have night terrors and has had them, on and off, ever since. The first time she had a night terror we didn't know what was going on. It's the most frightening experience to have your half-awake, half-asleep four-year-old child screaming in fear as she gazes past you at some object of terror visible to her only.

We have since discovered, to our relief, that it is a known phenomenon in a small number of children and that the best thing to do is not to try to shake her out of it, but to talk calmly to her and put a cold washer on her face. It soon passes and she goes back to sleep. We are told by a friend of ours who is a child psychologist that it might have been triggered by her brother's death.

❏ *Seven- to ten-year-olds*
This age group has progressed from interest in graves and funerals to interest in what happens after death. An eight- or nine-year-old is able to relate to some of the mysteries of death. This child is often beginning to think abstractly and can grasp the concept of a soul, so parents with religious convictions might like to introduce their beliefs about eternal life in more depth to their children at this stage.

However, children this age need a great deal of assurance and might feel insecure and vulnerable. They sometimes need to be told, 'No, Mummy and

Daddy are not going to die for a long, long time.'

You could find yourself thinking, 'How can I be certain when I will die?', but it is wiser not to pass on that uncertainty to your child at a time when what they need most is reassurance and comfort that their world, which has received a huge jolt, is not going to collapse completely. The passing of the years and a growing maturity will allow them to grapple with such weighty matters later when they are more emotionally able to cope.

❑ *Eleven- to fourteen-year-olds*
By this age, children are beginning to come to a much fuller understanding of the permanence of death. They know that the person won't be coming back. Often children this age have also been 'the other mother' and done many things a mother would do for a younger sibling. So they can be deeply affected by the death of a brother or sister.

When James died, the person who had held him most apart from Rosanne was Gracelyn, the eleven-year-old daughter of my boss at the time. She was shattered by his death, far more so than her sister Joy who was seven. Gracelyn was at the house within moments of our finding him and was able to hold him and cuddle him and say goodbye which I'm sure helped her grieve more fully.

However, the grief of children this age can be complicated by the fact that they are in transition from childhood to adulthood. One moment they will be acting very maturely, the next like a child. As they are trying to establish their own identity, they might find it easier to talk about their grief with their peers rather than their parents.

They also, like people of any age, might not express their anger directly. They sometimes suddenly explode in anger or become very emotional over a seemingly small matter. Often children this age will direct their anger about the death of their brother or sister at their parents, whom they hold partially responsible. You might also find yourself on the receiving end of anger that is really directed at God, but you're more accessible, so you get it.

❑ *Fifteen- to sixteen-year-olds*

Young people this age are generally more philosophical about life. They are going through that terrible but necessary process of finding out who they really are — 'Why are we here? Who am I? What, if anything, is the purpose of life?' This age group should be treated as adults in regard to grief and involved in everything that is happening as much as they want to be. You don't need to shelter them from the harsh realities of life because in the world we live in they have already been exposed to most of them.

The number one rule with all children of any age is to include them in your grief. Don't always send them off to Aunt Mary's. If you do, you will sow for yourselves a field of thorny questions which will be very difficult to answer later on because the child has not been allowed to be involved.

We were fortunate that Alice was with us when James was found. She went to the funeral and placed a small posy of flowers on James' casket.

She doesn't remember this, but it is something we've been able to build on.

If your child was not present at the time of death or immediately afterwards, you will have to work a lot harder at helping them come to terms with what has happened. Very often we respond to our children at such a stressful time out of our own fears and needs. You might well need to seek professional help to decide the best way to help children who were away at the time.

There is a deeply-held belief in our community that children are fragile little creatures who will be scarred for life if exposed to the terrible reality of death. But this is not true. Children are tougher than many adults and will often bounce back from tragedy much more quickly than we will.

Children are far more likely to be permanently scarred by being excluded from the family's grieving. If a child is usually included in family celebrations like birthdays and Christmas, but is excluded from the death, they might interpret it as punishment for having caused the situation. Children don't always understand death in an adult way, but they do understand a lot. Including them teaches them that tears, sadness and pain are all part of life and of the healing process.

You will sense when it is appropriate to let your children see you in tears and when it is not. If you have an especially bad patch and find yourself breaking down and crying very frequently and your children seem to be coping well with their own grief, it won't help them to find you in tears ten times a day. We must be careful not to burden our children with our own grief if they are coping well with theirs or to use them as a substitute spouse.

In the early days when we did a great deal of crying, we often did it together. Even now there are times when one of us cracks up and is discovered by another member of the family, which is usually a great comfort. What often sets me off is seeing a child who looks like I imagine James would now look or hearing about other children who have died. The television report of the Iraqi father who came home from the war in Kuwait to have his son die in his arms was too much for me. I ended in tears in front of the TV, but I did it in private.

It is also very important to let siblings talk about how they are feeling, even if it is painful or embarrassing for you. One day in a very quiet part of a church service, Alice decided to relay the entire story of James' death to a child in the next pew. She did so in a very loud voice which half the church must have been able to hear. Rosanne could have shut her up, but it was important for her to talk about it, so she let her go. Children sometimes want to go over and over the story, like adults, and this is all part of the grieving process. If you can bear it, let them go.

Children not only talk about how they are feeling; they also act out their grief. It may come out in very obvious ways or more subtly. Crying over a broken toy or a spoiled game might have little to do with the toy or the game and everything to do with their grief.

Another way of helping children work through their grief is to give them something concrete to do.

The three of us made a 'Life Book' for James. Together we planted a James Belton rhododendron a friend gave us in memory of James. We gave Alice her own photo of James in a frame which she still has on her dresser. We gave her a teddy my parents had given to James. We took her to the grave to put flowers on it and took photos of it.

Other people can also be helpful. Alice's grandparents spent quite a good deal of time with Alice after James died. They did lots of things with her, listened to her and gave her a great deal of reassurance. More than anything else, what a child who has had a brother or sister die needs to feel is loved. Later, when we began to remember some of the happy times, we helped her to remember some of them too.

So the things to remember are to include children in whatever way is appropriate, to let them express their feelings and to be more tolerant towards them.

4
Questions we ask

FROM THE MOMENT A CHILD WE LOVE DIES, we begin to question. The questions come pouring out of us. Why did my child die? What did we do wrong? Is God punishing me? Will our child go to heaven? We are searching for an answer. We are trying to make sense out of something that seems to make no sense.

The search for answers is not helped by the fact that most people who have had a child die find themselves on the receiving end of well-meaning cliches. People will attempt to comfort us by saying such things as: 'God only picks the most beautiful blossoms', or 'You're so lucky that you still have other children who are healthy'. Often Christians have scripture verses quoted to them like, 'All things work together for good to those who love the Lord.'

Someone who wrote to me recently said that some months after her child died, her parents expressed surprise she 'hadn't gotten over it yet'. At times people can give the impression that you should have no questions or doubts if you have faith in God.

Even if what is said is true, these kinds of comments are rarely helpful. They are things that those of us who have suffered such loss have to come to realise for ourselves in our own time and way. They can't be dropped on us by others who often are comforting themselves as much as they are us. Even the greatest truths can sound superficial and empty if applied as bandaids to a gaping wound. The death of a child is a bloody and gaping wound, which takes a long time to heal. And even after it has healed, a visible scar remains, which from time to time may reopen.

But it is essential that we work through our questions and doubts because only then can real healing come. I am aware that much of what I write in this chapter may sound like cliches to you if the death of your child was recent. I don't apologise for this, but simply trust that you will take what is helpful and ignore what is not.

When a person we love dies, we all need to hold someone responsible. That person may be our partner, but mostly it is God.

God questions

Whether we believe in God or not, most of us hold God responsible for the death of a loved one. This is especially so when it is a child who has died. In our hearts we feel that God is supposed to look after the young and the innocent — something rises up inside us in protest at the unfairness of their death: 'He was just starting out in life — it seems so unfair, so wrong.'

The first question almost everyone asks is, 'Why

me, God?' We assume that the death of our child is something that God has done to us — or at least allowed to happen. We may feel God is punishing us for something we have or haven't done.

If our picture of God is of a Being who rewards people for the good they do in this life and punishes them for the bad, then we may feel God has taken away our child to punish us.

Gerry's story is a case in point. He was consumed by guilt after his eleven-year-old son Christopher's accidental electrocution. Gerry was a top executive in a large manufacturing company which was expanding into South-East Asia, keeping him away for five of the last six months of his son's life. When he was at home, he was so tired and distracted that he'd spent little time with Christopher.

When Christopher was killed, he felt tremendous guilt and also that God was punishing him for having been a bad father. He felt that if he had spent more time at home and had done more with his son, Christopher might still have been alive.

'I can't get the thought out of my mind that God is paying me back for failing as a father,' he said. The idea that God rewards or punishes people for the things they do has been around for a long time.

Jesus addressed this issue when he met a man who had been blind from birth. His disciples asked him, 'Who sinned, this man or his parents? Why was he born blind?'

Jesus replied, 'Neither this man, nor his parents sinned.' The blindness was not caused by anything he or his parents had done. The God I believe in is not a God who punishes people by making them sick or causing them to die.

We live in a world where bad things happen. Innocent children die every day. In the time it has taken you to read this chapter, dozens of babies and children in Third World countries have starved to death. This is the kind of world we live in. When God made the world he had two choices. He could have created us all as robots who did everything he told us to, or he could have given us free will — which, the Bible tells us, is what he did.

Giving people free will instead of making them robots was risky. It meant that they had the freedom to choose to go the wrong way. The first book in the Bible, the book of Genesis, tells us that the first human beings chose to go their own way instead of God's way.

God wanted the people he created to have a relationship with him and to rely on him for all their needs. But instead they tried to live apart from God. This meant their relationship with God was broken, and disease and murder and death came into the world. It's not what God wanted for the human race, but that's the way it is.

When our child is one of the children to die, we can find ourselves questioning the goodness of God. How can God just sit back and let these things happen? At first we may not realise that it is God's goodness that we are questioning, but it is. If we didn't believe God was a good God, we would have no right to question his goodness. If God was evil, then it would be consistent with his character to make bad things happen to people.

It is because we believe in his *goodness* that we

have a problem with the seemingly senseless death of our children. So how can a good God allow such evil and suffering?

This is a question with which the great religious thinkers and philosophers of the world have grappled for centuries. There are no neat solutions to such complex problems. One solution would be not to believe in the existence of God at all. If the world we live in came to be by accident or chance and there was no Designer, then the problem is solved. There is no point in asking why evil and suffering exist because there is no point to evil and suffering. There is no reason or purpose for them. They just are.

Another solution is to see God as a clockmaker who, having made the clock of the universe, set it ticking and left it to its own devices. This God watches from the sidelines, but never interferes in human affairs.

A Jewish writer, Rabbi Harold Kushner, says something similar to this in his book *When Bad Things Happen to Good People*. He believes that, because God has given us free will, he is not able to influence events on earth. God is powerless to do anything about human suffering and pain. We must battle along on our own as best we can.

Yet another way some people try to solve the problem is to believe that God has worked out who will die and when and how. It is all predestined and there is nothing any of us can do about it. All we can do is grit our teeth and bear it.

My experience has been that this is the sort of thing many people believe. I've lost count of the number of times a bereaved person has told me, 'Oh well, it must have been the will of God, otherwise it wouldn't have happened.' Whatever will be will be and there's nothing you can do but accept it. Often people are comforted by the thought that even though something terrible has happened, God was responsible for making it happen.

Another way of understanding the problem is to believe that, while God has given human beings free will, he still at times intervenes in human history. He is watching what is happening on earth and is very concerned for our welfare. In fact, God was so concerned for us that he became a human being, in the person of the man Jesus, and lived on earth and died to mend the broken relationship between God and the human race.

Those who accept this view, which is the one put forward in the Bible, believe that because Jesus was really human he experienced the pain, suffering and isolation that we all at times experience. This doesn't solve the problem of why bad things happen to good people, but it does mean — if you believe it — that God didn't just sit back and watch human suffering from a distance. He actually experienced it for himself at first hand. He suffered the pain of watching his own son die and he still suffers today when we suffer. If God could suffer, then so could anyone.

And this leads me to the 'Why me?' question I raised. I must be honest and say that when our son died, my first response was not 'Why me?' In fact, it was more 'Why *not* me?' We live in a world where death is the one absolute certainty. It can come to us or those we love at any age, at any time, in any place. None of us are immune, no matter how much money we have, how famous we are, or how many prayers we've said.

While I don't understand why God continues to allow disease, war and tragic accidents that take innocent young lives, I believe it must be necessary.

I will nail my colours clearly to the mast here and say that I believe in a good God. I believe in a good God, despite the death of our son James and the deaths of so many others which seem to make no sense. I believe, in faith, that evil must be necessary in the purpose and plan of God, because if it wasn't he couldn't allow it to continue to exist.

Let me try to explain more clearly with these words from C.S. Lewis' book, *A Grief Observed*, about the suffering of his wife Joy, when she was dying of cancer. He writes: 'But is it credible that such extremities of torture should be necessary for us? Well, take your choice. The tortures occur. If they are unnecessary, then there is no God or a bad one. If there is a good God, then these tortures are necessary. For no even moderately good Being could possibly inflict or permit them if they weren't.'

Another important question many parents have, but most are afraid to ask, is whether it is wrong to be angry at God. The reason most people are afraid to admit they are angry at God is that they have been told it's a sin.

Recently when I was hospital visiting, I met a patient who said he wanted nothing to do with me. One said, 'I know who you are, mate, and I don't want to know you.' I sensed real anger behind his words, which I suspect was probably more directed at the God he saw me representing than at me.

When people we love die, we can feel very angry at God. Why did he let it happen? Why didn't he do something? We feel that God is to blame.

I once met a man called Ted in hospital who was very angry with God. Ted told me that in a period of fifteen months, his wife, his father, his only son and his brother had all died. He said that while he wasn't a churchgoer, he believed in God. And because he believed in God, he held him responsible for what had happened.

'I am so angry at God for doing this to me. I know I'm not a churchgoer, but I'm not a bad person either. I try hard to do the right thing by people. So why has God done this to me?'

Ted went on to say that his next-door neighbour was a regular churchgoer and that, after his wife and father died, he had talked to her about how he was feeling. He had told her how angry he felt towards God and she had told him that he shouldn't be talking like that. She said it was wrong to be angry at God and that he should repent of his sins before something else happened.

Then Ted's son was killed and he said he began to hate God. I listened to what Ted had to say and could have wept. I felt angry about what had happened to him and I felt angry with his next-door neighbour. I didn't say anything except to ask if he'd like me to go back and see him again, which he said he would.

When I went back, I listened again to his story.

Then I said I believed it was okay to feel angry at God. In fact, I told him I believed that he should tell God about his anger.

I told him the story of our son's death, about how angry I had become with God after James died, about what I had been told — that God can cope with our anger because he has broad shoulders. God isn't so small and petty that he stamps off in a huff because one of his creatures dares tell him they're angry with him. He didn't say much, but I could see he was taking it in.

The next time I saw him he told me that he had gone to an isolated beach and spent a good hour shouting his anger at God. He said he was still angry with God, but that he had stopped hating him. He was on the road to a more real relationship with God and had removed a lot of anger and resentment from his system.

Anger is a normal reaction to the death of a child. But it can become a problem if we fail to express it or if we become so locked into our anger that it colours our whole lives. We may at times feel angry with everyone and everything, but if that anger becomes a permanent state, we have a real problem. Later we deal with ways to channel anger positively.

Heaven questions

Another question almost all parents ask is: 'Will my child go to heaven?' I know some people argue that unless the parents of the dead child are Christians, or unless the child has made a commitment to Christ, they won't go to heaven.

But what about children who were too young to

choose? There are a number of incidents in the Bible which are relevant here.

Once some mothers brought their children to Jesus for him to bless. The disciples of Jesus knew how tired he was and tried to stop them. But Jesus said, 'Let the little children come to me, and don't hinder them, for the kingdom of heaven belongs to small children like these.' Jesus saw that the simple trust of children helped them to get nearer to God than anyone else.

How often our children amaze us with their comments about God. Because they accept that he exists and he loves them, they are able to trust God in a way that often we as sophisticated adults cannot. Jesus responds to this simple trust by putting his hands on their heads and blessing them. I believe that what he did with these children on earth he also does for them in heaven. The Lord accepts and receives our dead children into his Father's house.

I have no hesitation in assuring the parents of children who have died that I believe they are safe in heaven with God. But I can't tell them any more than that because the Bible doesn't tell us any more. We don't know whether they stay the same age or whether they grow at the same rate they would have on earth or whether they are ageless. We don't know whether they will look the same.

For months after James died, the thing we most wanted was to hold him in our arms. We still do. But we'll have to wait for heaven to know if we'll be able to. I hope so.

We don't know what our children are doing or if

they can see us and what we're doing. It would be easy to say, 'It doesn't matter. It's enough to know that they're safe with God.' But if you're the parent of a child who has died, you'll know it does matter very much. We're just as concerned for the welfare of our son now as we were when he was alive.

Sometimes parents are concerned their children may not have gone to heaven because they weren't christened. Often if babies are sick, parents will ask for them to be baptised in case they die. In the past there has been a belief that christening is a way of making sure your children get into heaven. There is nothing in scripture to support this belief.

Will God refuse to allow a baby into heaven because it 'hasn't been done'? Baptism isn't magic. It's a sign of the entry of the Spirit of God into a person's life, but it is not an automatic guarantee of salvation.

Whether or not an older person who has had the chance to accept or reject Christ will be accepted into heaven is another issue: the Bible makes it clear that faith in Jesus is necessary for entry into God's kingdom. But we are talking here about a child who has never had the opportunity to accept or reject Jesus as the Lord of their life. I believe the clear message of scripture is that, whether or not a child has been christened, God in his love will welcome them into heaven.

I have recently come across several parents who have been tempted to try to make contact with their dead child through a clairvoyant or medium. I understand why a grieving parent would want to do this, but believe that it may not be helpful. Even were a parent to believe he was able to get in touch with the spirit of his dead child, this kind of action can only delay the grieving process.

If you analyse why you want to try to contact your dead child in this way, you will find that you are really trying to bring them back or at least hold onto them. But they are dead. Nothing you do can bring them back. That's the harsh reality and we need to accept it if we are going to get on with life. The alternative is to deny the reality of what has happened, which I believe only leads to despair.

There is also a danger that such contact with the occult will allow evil forces into our lives. The Bible warns again and again that this spiritual realm is an area we should never venture into. Even if we do so for seemingly right motives, love for a dead child, we may find that things get out of control.

The first king of Israel, Saul, once used a medium to call up the spirit of the dead prophet Samuel. It cost him his kingship and, in the end, his life. As grieving parents, we have enough emotional trauma to work through without opening our lives to spiritual forces that may harm us or our families.

Medical questions

As I said at the start of this chapter, we all need to hold someone responsible for our child's death. This leads us to search for reasons and causes.

It may be that the death of your child was caused, or appeared to have been caused, because of a mistake by a member of the medical profession. Members of the medical profession are only human, despite our desire as a community to treat them as gods. Doctors and nurses make mistakes like all of us and, if they work in areas of critical care, sometimes those mistakes can be fatal.

We know of a case of a child whose heart stopped during an emergency appendix operation and, for whatever reason, no action was taken to revive him for five minutes. By then irreversible brain damage had been done and he lapsed into a coma. He died two weeks later. In a clear-cut case like this, the parents were told they would probably be successful if they sued the doctors and the hospital. But after a great deal of thought, they decided not to sue because they felt that no amount of money would bring their son back to life.

If there are doubts in your mind about the role medication may have played in the death of your child, it is probably best to explore those doubts rather than ignore them. For example, Ray and Marie, whose sixteen-week-old baby girl died a cot death, felt they had to fully explore the medical question. Just before their daughter Christy died, Marie had been in hospital for an operation. She had taken Christy to hospital with her and, after she died, had been very worried that this had in some way contributed to her death.

Marie had also been on pain killers following the operation and had taken a sleeping tablet the night before her daughter died. Her fear was that some of the medication could have been passed on to Christy because she was being breastfed. She told Ray about her fears and they decided they wanted to do all they could to discover whether Marie's medication could have contributed to her death. Even if it had contributed, they felt they would rather have the truth. They spoke to their GP and also the surgeon who performed Marie's operation.

They were told it was possible a small amount of the medication could have affected their daughter, but that the amount would have been so small that it would not have in any way contributed to her death.

Marie and Ray said they were relieved and pleased they had checked it out instead of just feeling guilty. My feeling is that the more questions you can answer about the death of your child the better.

After James died, we decided we wanted to find out more medically about his death. The local SIDS counseller told us we could ask for a copy of James' autopsy report, which we requested from the coroner. We were warned the report would be graphic and it was.

We coped well until we read that his stomach contained a large amount of breast milk. But we had decided it was better to know the facts than to imagine what had happened. We had also been told that the local pathologist was happy to discuss the post-mortem with parents, so we made an appointment to see him. He was very helpful and did his best to answer our questions.

Somehow it was comforting to speak to the person who had performed the autopsy on our son's body. We didn't learn any more about why he had died, but we left feeling much happier. But this is a very personal matter. We are all different and we need to do what feels right for us.

Also, it will depend on how cooperative your local authorities are. While it is your right to have a copy of the autopsy, you may find that some coroners are less than willing to provide you with one. If that happens, whether you succeed in getting what you want or not will depend entirely on how determined you are.

It is not your right to have an interview with the pathologist who conducted the autopsy. This will depend on the openness and cooperation of the individual concerned. But if you make your request politely, most pathologists will comply. Let's face it, it's not easy for a professional to sit down with the parents of a child whose body he has cut open and calmly discuss the results. If he or she feels they may be subjected to the parents' anger or aggression, they are not likely to agree to such an interview.

By the end of the interview, the pathologist who had performed James' autopsy was visibly upset. I admire any pathologist who is willing to take the time to sit down with parents and help them in this way, because it costs them. Most of them are probably parents, too.

5
Reality sets in

SOONER OR LATER YOUR FEELINGS OF NUMBNESS will begin to wear off. For the first weeks or months you will swing between feeling that what has happened is a nightmare which will go away if only you wait long enough, and knowing that it is only too real and will not go away. But the time will come when your times of knowing it is real will outnumber your times of feeling it is a nightmare.

This is a sign that you are beginning to accept what has happened. You may begin to think about what should be done with your child's clothes or toys or books. You may find yourself wanting to look at a photograph of your child, which is something you could never have done when your grief was raw.

You may find yourself going over and over the events that took place before the death of your child. This often happens because your mind is working on it, trying to find an answer. When we have a child die, our mind tries to provide us with a rational answer as to why our child died, there is no answer, or at least not one that will satisfy us.

Such an answer is beyond the capacity of the human mind. In this life the death of our child will remain a mystery. Even if we know exactly how they died, we cannot know why. Often this searching for an answer can lead us into guilt and blame.

Work on relationships

Many relationships where a child has died break down irretrievably. There is nothing more destructive of human relationships than blame.

When one of our children dies, we are overwhelmed with feelings of guilt. We go over and over the events surrounding the death of our child, looking for someone to hold responsible, someone to blame. We almost certainly blame ourselves, to some degree, and we may also blame our partner. The blame may be justified, in the sense that our partner did something which caused or contributed to the death of our child, or it may not.

Clive and Geraldine had four children. They had taken their children to a seaside resort for a holiday at the beach. All of their children were good swimmers except the second youngest, Chris, who for some reason did not like the water very much.

One afternoon Geraldine had gone into town to do some shopping. She says that before she left she felt uneasy about leaving the children at the beach with Clive. They all decided to go for a swim and Clive sat under a beach umbrella reading. There was a floating diving platform about a hundred metres offshore which they decided to swim out to and dive from. Chris didn't want to go, but his younger sister urged him.

Clive overheard this conversation, but decided not to intervene because he felt that Chris, who was eleven, was old enough to decide for himself.

Chris made it out to the platform safely. But on the way back he suddenly developed severe cramp. He called out for help, but by the time his elder brothers reached him he had gone under. They screamed to their father for help and he immediately swam out to them. They began diving for their brother but, by the time they found him and dragged him to the surface, he was blue. With their father's help they got Chris in to shore and began mouth-to-mouth resuscitation and external heart massage.

Tragically, although they managed to get him breathing and his heart going again, he was severely brain damaged. He was rushed to intensive care, given the best medical treatment available, but died three weeks later.

The entire family was guilt-ridden. Geraldine felt she should never have gone shopping — that if she'd stayed, Chris wouldn't have gone swimming and would still be alive. Clive couldn't forgive himself for having said nothing to stop Chris going swimming. His brothers felt they should have been able to get to him more quickly and his sister felt she had caused his death by urging him to go.

The long-term effect on Clive and Geraldine's twenty-two-year relationship was devastating. They kept going over and over the events of that afternoon, but neither was able to express how they really felt. Privately, Geraldine blamed Clive for their son's death: 'He was the responsible adult on that occasion. He was in charge of the children. He should have prevented Chris' death!' Clive also blamed himself. He sensed his wife's unspoken feelings and they only made him feel more guilty.

Over the next twelve months, Geraldine's resentments over her son's death began to poison their marriage. Finally, they realised what a bad state their marriage was in and went to marriage guidance counselling, but it was too late. The damage had already been done and they separated. They are now divorced. Geraldine has remarried and Clive is under constant psychiatric care.

Clive and Geraldine's marriage was, according to their friends and family, a good one. It is not true to say that only shaky relationships break down. *Any* relationship will collapse if the couple concerned stop communicating.

The key is to keep communicating, keep talking, even if our talking is telling our partner how angry we are at them or how frustrated we are feeling. But this does not mean attacking our partner. Instead of saying, 'You make me feel so angry!' which is attacking them as a person and not accepting responsibility for your own reactions, it is better to say, 'When you say things like that it makes me feel so angry.' This helps us to keep the lines of communication open instead of having it develop into a full-scale argument that goes nowhere. Tell your partner how you are feeling.

There is no need to be afraid to seek out professional help. There is nothing shameful about admitting that a relationship is in trouble. Most couples I know who are honest will admit they have problems they need to work on in their relationship.

This is especially true of parents who have had a child die. Bereavement can put pressure on areas of our relationship that were already in trouble. But surely if our relationships are worth having, they are worth investing in and fighting for.

I believe that many marriages break down simply because those in them fail to understand that relationships in this life are hard work which require a great deal of time, effort and energy. We wouldn't dream of expecting a home to build itself magically for us brick by brick and board by board with no real effort on our part.

And yet that is so often the way we approach complex intimate relationships. We give a great deal of money and hard work to buy or build ourselves a home — those of us who can still afford it. But relationships are no different. In fact, they require far more work than building a home.

Allow ourselves to express grief

Twenty years ago, after the death of a child, it was generally the father who would return to work within about a week and the mother would stay home. This meant that men often delayed their grieving or put it off permanently. But women stayed in the same environment in which they had cared for their children. Home was a constant reminder to them of their dead child and, whilst they could escape it for a while, it was always there to come back to.

This meant they tended to do a lot more crying, but it also meant they tended to deal with their grief more healthily. There was no running away from it in most cases.

But now many women also return to work immediately after the death of a child which means they also often postpone their grieving. This is why it is so important to make time to express our grief — more will be said about this in the next chapter.

Despite the revolution in the workplace, the roles of men and women have not changed a great deal in many ways. There is still an expectation that men will be tough. Very few men in Western society are able to let their feelings out. We have been conditioned from an early age to hold our emotions in and that is what most of us do. Few men are in touch with their 'feminine' side. We are often afraid to learn more about that part of us for fear of being thought weak or discovering that we are homosexual.

Women on the other hand are expected to cry — 'That is what women are like!' If you fail to cry as a bereaved mother, you may well find yourself being labelled 'tough', usually behind your back. Women, of course, are never meant to be tough. That is the province of men.

I believe we must do all we can to break down these stereotypes. There is nothing weak about expressing emotion in public. Men from other cultures are able to show their feelings in public, whether at soccer or funerals, without being labelled weak. As Western men we could learn from them.

We also need to recognise that personality plays an important role in the way a person grieves. If you are an introvert, you may find it extremely difficult to show your emotions in public. Bursting into tears in the middle of a shopping complex for no apparent reason may be an acutely embarrassing experience. If you are a very private person, the last thing you may want the day after your child died is a house full of people all expressing their condolences. You may want only to crawl into a hole and stay there. And for you that may be quite a healthy thing to do.

We need to know what kind of person we are and remain true to ourselves in the midst of our pain. I am an extrovert and having a house full of people the day after our son died was, for me, a great comfort. I am not saying that all extroverts can easily grieve in public and that introverts find it difficult, but we should be aware that personality affects the way we grieve.

Beware of the pitfalls if you are a Christian

There are special dangers for Christians in working through the death of a child. Very often Christians are expected to respond to the death of a child differently from someone who is not a Christian.

The thinking goes something like this: 'Christians believe in life after death. Therefore, because of your faith, you can be certain your child is safe. So you need not grieve too deeply or stay upset too long because of the death of your child.' We were fortunate that very few people treated us in this way when James died but, sadly, we have spoken to many parents who have been treated in this way.

This kind of thinking is both naive and unrealistic. I believe it is unchristian. Certainly Christians believe life goes on beyond death, but because they have this faith, it doesn't mean they cease to be people who feel grief and pain. Being a Christian who believes in an existence beyond this life isn't some magic protection against feeling pain and loss.

We know of a couple in Melbourne who had a twin die when he was seven-and-a-half weeks old. Some months later, when visiting their parents, they said how much they were still hurting over the death of their son. The parents' response was, 'But you're Christians', as if that meant they should be all over it.

Christians have great comfort in knowing where their child is and with whom. But the sense of loss can be just as great, because while we believe we will see them again, we know it will not be in this life.

However, I don't want to belittle the power of prayer, especially the prayers of others at times of crisis in our lives. After James died, we felt surrounded by the prayers of people all over Australia. We were very aware of God's love and strength flowing to us through the prayers of others. At times it was almost a physical warmth.

But we shouldn't expect that such strength and comfort will enable us to shrug off our grief lightly or easily. The experience of Christians through the ages has been that God will be with them in the midst of the trauma, no matter how terrible it is. God didn't stop the apostle Paul from being shipwrecked, imprisoned or even dying for his faith in Christ, but he was alongside him through all those experiences to give him the strength he needed.

Grief is a journey which everyone who has had a loved one die must make, no matter what they believe about God. So if you are a Christian, don't be too hard on yourself. Allow yourself to grieve and let it all out.

Jesus cried bitterly when his friend Lazarus died. He wasn't afraid to show his emotions. If it was good enough for him, it's good enough for those of us who follow him.

God doesn't see tears as weakness or a lack of faith. He invented them, in the same way he created the rain, which when it falls on the earth washes it clean. Tears are God's gift to help wash away some of our hurt and pain. Of course this applies to everyone, not only those who call themselves Christians.

Be willing to reassess values

Most people who have a child die find it changes their life dramatically. It is an event which turns life upside down. It causes most people to reassess their values — what they really believe.

Listen to the thoughts of Catherine, five weeks after her four-year-old daughter accidentally hanged herself:

> I remember wandering aimlessly for hours on the beach and along the country backroads near our home. One morning I got up at dawn and walked down to the beach.
> It was one of those beautiful clear blue-skied mornings — not a cloud in the sky and so still. There was a seagull flying so high it was almost out of sight. The waves lapped gently on the sand. It was so peaceful. I remember being overwhelmed

by the realisation of what a precious gift life is, that every moment of every day is to be treasured and savoured because we never know how long we'll have it. How often I'd taken it all for granted.

I recall having very similar feelings after James died. Life is too precious to take for granted. Just over a year after James died Rosanne and I attended the National Sudden Infant Death Syndrome (SIDS) Conference in Brisbane, a superbly organised event. We had the wonderful opportunity of not only hearing the latest research on cot death, but also spending time with other parents whose children had died.

I vividly remember sitting in one seminar with another SIDS father, from Queensland. The person leading the session, an Anglican priest, shared how his son had died at the age of fifteen. Tears came into the eyes of the man sitting next to me and into mine, too. We ended the seminar hugging one another and weeping together, as two fathers who had both had sons die.

We spoke to a large number of parents whose children had died and almost all of them said the same thing: 'We feel better people because of what we've had to work through since our children died.'

The experience had changed their lives in a positive way.

Sadly this is often not the case. Many relationships break down after the death of a child. When this happens, it is very often because people have held their grief in instead of letting it out and so are unable to accept the possibility of change that might have come from open grief.

Deal with any unfinished business from the past

Often a bereavement will trigger off other undealt-with grief in a person's life. The particular loss is a catalyst to bring all the pain and hurt from past griefs to the surface.

I remember one person in particular whose spouse had died suddenly and tragically. She was totally overwhelmed by her grief to the point where she found it hard to function. She realised as time passed that this particular grief had brought to the surface two other major griefs — the death of her father thirty years earlier and the effects of a traumatic incident involving a child.

It was almost as if these griefs had continued to exist in their hermetically sealed compartments because they had been repressed, but had continued to affect the way she was living her life. The death of her spouse had tipped the balance and all the griefs came pouring out together. Because she had someone who was prepared to listen —literally for days — the griefs were dealt with and she, in time, resumed a relatively normal life.

The value of such support and outpouring can hardly be overestimated in such cases.

Be aware that sickness comes from holding grief in

One of the major effects of holding grief in is sickness.

We are coming to understand a great deal more about the relationship between grief and sickness. Physical sickness is very often a manifestation of emotional or mental trauma. Because there is 'disease' in the mind, it affects the body. There is mounting evidence that repression of strong emotions like anger and resentment can cause physical sickness and mental breakdown.

The Old Testament book of Proverbs says, 'As a person thinks, so they are.' In other words, if we fill our mind with anger, that is what we will become — someone whose life is full of anger. It is very likely that our anger will manifest itself in our life in some physical way.

Canon Jim Glennon, a man with a lifetime's involvement in the healing ministry, tells how a man who once came to him with the story of a deep and continued disagreement with a work colleague. The man, called Bob, had shown a generous attitude towards this particular person in his business relationship, only to discover that he had been used. It didn't happen just once, but a number of times, to the point where Bob developed a real resentment towards this man. This resentment caused a rift in both their personal and business relationships.

About two years later, Bob began to notice a large area of discolouration on his neck which medical examination revealed to be a form of skin cancer. It was a pre-cancerous condition which could be effectively treated, but would leave unsightly scars. There was quite a delay before the operation, which gave Bob the time to reflect on life and especially his feelings towards this former business colleague, who had by then moved interstate.

After much thought, he decided he wanted to put their relationship right. He wrote to him, addressing him by his first name which he had never done before, saying he regretted the trouble between them and asking for forgiveness for his faults in the matter. It was the first time he had expressed any regret over what had happened because, until then, he had felt it was all the other man's fault.

The man wrote back also expressing regret about what had happened and admitting for the first time his own failure and guilt. Shortly after this, the skin cancer disappeared without any medical treatment and did not come back.

This does not mean that everyone who represses their resentment or anger or grief will become physically ill, but it does highlight the fact that there is often a link between our emotions and our health. Rosanne and I both had arthritis in our hands for several months after James' death for no explicable reason. But it seemed to be a physical outworking of our grieving.

Even if we don't repress our feelings as grieving parents, we may experience all kinds of physical reactions to the death of our child. But if we do repress our emotions, current research seems to indicate that those physical reactions will last longer and be more severe.

Understand the reasons for possible sexual problems

This disharmony or dis-ease may well affect our sexual relationship. Some people may feel they need more physical comfort — cuddling and touching — than usual. This is a common reaction in the early days after the death of a child.

I can still vividly remember the first few nights after James' death when we clung to each other to get to sleep. There was great comfort in being that close.

But often in the longer term there may be a negative effect on the sexual relationship. From a woman's point of view, this is hardly surprising. The parts of her body involved in sexual intercourse are also those connected with child-bearing. The act of intercourse is inevitably a reminder not only of conception, but also of pregnancy and childbirth. For some women this may be too painful emotionally, perhaps even physically, in those early days.

While sex may be a helpful distraction for a man, it may be nothing but painful memories for a woman. Sexual problems after the death of a child are common.

Men especially need to show consideration and a great deal of patience towards their partners in the months following the death of a child. If either one, or perhaps both of you, continues to have problems in this area, seek professional counselling straight away.

Terry and Gaye had had a very active sexual relationship until the death of their seven-year-old son in a hit-and-run accident. But his death stopped their sex life overnight. Gaye recalls:

> I was so upset in those first few days, I couldn't even think straight enough to make myself a cup of tea, let alone make love. All I could think about was Robbie.
>
> Terry was very understanding for the first week, but then he started insisting that he needed sex. He

said it would help him to forget. I told him all it would do for me would be to make me remember and that he'd just have to wait.

We had a few very tense weeks and I remember once, after a full-scale row, he blurted out that if he couldn't get what he needed at home he'd have to go and get it somewhere else. That started me thinking and I realised I'd have to start responding to his advances. The first time was the hardest, but after a while our sex life got back to normal and everything was okay.

This demonstrates the sorts of problems that can arise. If either of you, or perhaps both of you, continues to have problems in this area, seek professional help as quickly as possible. It may save your relationship.

6
Letting it out

IF I HAVE LEARNED ANYTHING on the journey of grief, it is that we must let our feelings out. How we do it is not important. What is important is that we do it.

The inability to let our feelings out can be very destructive. I have met so many people who are living crippled and often bitterly unhappy lives, because they have failed to express their feelings of grief and pain. This chapter contains a wide range of ways of getting our grief out.

Talking it out

One of the best ways I know of dealing with grief is simply talking about it. Talk about how you are feeling. If you're feeling angry or frustrated or down, tell someone.

Obviously you need to pick who you tell and when. Five minutes before your husband is due to leave for work may not be the best time to unload. Your partner may not always be the best person to talk to. Find someone you can trust and tell them exactly how you're feeling. If you can't find anyone to talk to, make use of one of the excellent counselling services we have at our disposal, like *Lifeline*.

Sometimes it may be much easier to talk to a stranger than someone you know. After James died, I found talking very therapeutic. I talked a great deal to Rosanne and to several other close friends.

I also talked to God. There were times when I found myself becoming angry with God because James' death seemed so unfair. I had longed to have a son and after only nine weeks he had been taken away. It seemed so wrong. But my faith in God allowed me to become angry with him. God is my heavenly Father. Prayer can be a wonderful resource to help us let out our feelings of grief.

I talk to God about everything. I tell him exactly how I feel. God is big enough to cope with our most intense emotions and thoughts. I say I told God how angry I was, but I didn't *stay* angry with him. Having told him about my anger, there came a time when my feelings of anger began to subside.

If I had stayed angry with God permanently, I think it would have seriously damaged my relationship with him and I wasn't prepared to do that. I had to let the anger out, but in the end I chose to trust, in faith, that what I cannot understand at the moment I will one day understand.

That doesn't mean that there are not still times when I feel angry with God, but when I weigh my anger against my faith, my faith wins.

Writing it out

Not all of us are talkers. In fact, some people find it very hard to talk about their emotions. Another more private way of expressing our grief is writing. The advantage of writing is that no-one else need ever see it or even know it exists, unless of course you decide to write a book, in which case your writing will become very public!

Writing is a wonderful way of expressing our feelings of grief. It helps us sort through our emotions as we write. There is something in the process of writing words down which helps us to deal with the feelings behind the words.

Another advantage of writing is that we can look back on it and check our progress on the journey of grief. Malcolm kept a journal after the death of his daughter on the advice of a grief counsellor he met at the hospital. He says:

> I was amazed as I looked back twelve months after Judy died to see how my grief had changed in that time. The first entries just after Judy died were raw. I was spilling my guts all over the pages. I'm not usually an emotional kind of guy. But boy did I let it all out in that book!
>
> My writing during those first few months was all guilt and regret, but gradually I began to write about a few of the wonderful family times we'd had and I could feel some of the pain beginning to ease. I'm still writing now two-and-a-half years later. It's been great therapy. Thank God for that counsellor who put me onto it in the first place.

Sheryl also wrote down her feelings, eight months after the death of her one-and-a-half-year-old son Patrick. She had just given birth to another son, Hamish:

> I think of Patrick every day and wonder what it would be like now with three little boys. How I hate the fact that Patrick died and I hate the fact that his body is rotting in the ground. Sometimes I feel that cremation would have been better, but I would not wish that we had done it any other way.
>
> For some time now I have felt that most people do not want to hear me talk about Patrick, but I would so much like more opportunities to talk about him, go over his photos and talk about how I feel now. I am writing this because I would so much like an opportunity to talk about how I feel now — the sorrow, the pain, the hurt, the sense of loss, the four-year gap.
>
> Also the fear of another son dying, the protective feelings towards Hamish. Am I going to be over-protective? I wonder about the future — plan a little and dare to feel happier. Will those happier feelings be shattered? I would so much like to talk to someone about how I feel now, but everyone seems busy with their own lives and I don't feel I should intrude with my needs.

Sheryl felt a great need to talk to someone about her feelings, but there was no-one to talk to, so she wrote down the way she felt. This is the wonderful thing about writing. It is like talking to someone. In some ways it is even better because you then have the record to look back on.

In her writing, Sheryl picks up what is often a big problem after the first few weeks:

> So many people were around initially and in the week following, but now we are left with our sorrow and pain. I feel such a need to talk about my

feelings and hopes for Hamish. The death of a child is so painful and invasive. It stops me feeling content.

Sometimes I start to feel more content again and then I feel that something will shatter that feeling. No longer can I plan and hope the way I used to, expecting that I and my loved ones will live out our three score years and ten. The death of a child knocks over self-confidence, self-esteem, expectancy of life — and interferes with attitudes towards a new son.

Many people, as well as keeping a diary or journal, also write poetry to express their innermost feelings. This can be a helpful thing to do.

Out of the raw grief and agony of James' death I wrote these words:

I can see him still as I found him — unmoving, lifeless, close-lidded. From the crucible of agony — a wordless cry. It rends our beings. Our heart, still pumping, has been ripped from our bodies, leaving a trail of blood. The joys and smiles, hopes and dreams lie dead, like him, at our feet. He is not here. He is no longer with us. The smile-bringer lies in the earth, cold and still, all smiles gone now, his life-blood drained away.

We cry for a miracle. We long for a Lazarine restoration, almost more than life itself. But it does not come. And our hearts ache for all who have passed this way before.

Little did we know. Nothing did we know. Father forgive us. Words are like paper cups strewn around the field of play and blown by the wind, empty and worse than useless. Acts of love and devotion erode the wall of numbness and hold us this side of sanity, but only just.

Please, no platitudes, no answers, no well-meaning advice. Not now, maybe never. Leave us alone to grieve for our little boy.

The flame of hope burns yet, but only dimly. It sizzles and splutters under the gushing, unending torrent of grief. It falters and flickers under the waterfall of our tears. It almost goes out, but somehow burns on. He is not here. He is no longer with us. He is far beyond us, beyond hurt and pain and fear, beyond our outstretched hands and our aching hearts, but not beyond the arms of Love.

You may feel that you could never write down your thoughts and feelings on paper like this. But have you ever tried it? The artistic merit of such writing is irrelevant. We don't do it for others. We do it for ourselves. If our writing is helpful to others, that's good; but it's primarily for us, not them.

If you would like some help in writing down your grief journey, there is an excellent book we came across at the Brisbane SIDS Conference called *Coming to New Life*. It is a grief journal and it guides us through our journey of grief from the beginning.

It begins by asking us to write down the story of our loss, the people involved, every relevant detail. Then it helps us put our loss into perspective, relates it to earlier losses and looks more deeply at the role of feelings in grieving.

This workbook deals with such matters as anger, depression, suicide and guilt. It has a very good section on children and grief and some excellent suggestions on how to help them cope with death. But the best thing about this book is that it gets us writing down our thoughts and feelings.

I lent our copy to a nursing sister friend who works with the Stillbirth and Neonatal Death Support (SANDS). She used it with both maternity nursing staff and parents of stillborn babies and said that everyone who worked through the journal found it very helpful.

Letting the anger out

Anger is a normal part of grieving. That doesn't mean you must feel angry about the death of your child. You are not abnormal if you don't feel anger about your child's death, but you are probably an exception. Most people feel angry sooner or later. You may know exactly why you feel angry or you may feel angry at everything and everyone and have no idea why. Mostly at the root of our anger is the cry of our hearts: 'This just isn't fair!'

I have few problems letting my anger out. As my family well knows, I am the sort of person who is much more likely to give other people ulcers than get them myself. While I rarely take my anger out on people, I vent it on things — doors, for instance.

I will remember as long as I live the day I kicked out at the duck. We had acquired two Muscovy ducks a few months before James died. In a rather beautiful act of providence, the female managed to produce about fifteen eggs a day or so after James' death — one of the few signs of hope for the future around at the time. We waited with excitement to see how many ducklings would hatch. Six fluffy little balls of duckling struggled into the world and waddled around the backyard behind mother.

One very wet day, she decided that instead of keeping her two-day-old progeny safe and dry under cover, she would parade them around the backyard. I was infuriated by this — I'd been told by our local parish duck expert that ducklings didn't grow down which would protect them from the wet until they were three or four days old.

I rushed into the backyard to encourage the stupid duck to get her kids back under shelter. She was stubborn — the more I tried to get her out of the rain, the more determined she seemed to be to stay where she was. Finally, out of sheer frustration, I did a very unchristian, unanimal-loving thing: I kicked her — or at least I aimed a kick at her, hoping that it would force her in out of the rain. Fortunately I missed, but it had the desired effect and she speedily ushered her little ones back to the safety of shelter.

Rosanne thought I had gone crazy — the poor duck! — and it wasn't until I had time to reflect on the event that I realised *why* I had reacted so strongly. I saw the duck as a parent acting irresponsibly to the young she had in her care and that made me angry.

I still sometimes feel anger towards parents who appear to be mistreating their children. I have often felt like walking up to parents blowing smoke into the faces of their young babies and saying, 'Do you realise you may kill your baby if you keep blowing smoke into its lungs like that?' (Smoking during and after pregnancy is one of the major factors in cot death.)

As you have probably already realised, dealing with anger isn't my strong point. It's something I am constantly working on. Many men, in my experience, have a problem with anger. I used to think I didn't have a real problem with it because I let it out, but I've realised that my letting it out has a negative effect on those who are in the vicinity when I do it.

One thing I have learned is that my anger is almost always the symptom, not the cause of the problem. My anger is a response to something else that is happening to me. If I can deal with that, I can usually overcome the anger. In the case of James' death, I had to work through resentment and bitterness towards certain people before my anger went. I needed to forgive them for what I believed they had done and ask God to forgive me for having felt that way towards them. When I did that, the anger went.

In *Coming to New Life*, John Chalmers has some helpful points on anger:

> Anger is like an atomic bomb: it can sit innocuously inside someone and then suddenly explode, causing devastation everywhere, destroying itself and lots of people nearby. . . Here are some healthy ways of channelling the raw energy of anger:
> * Play an energetic game of squash, tennis, handball — mentally imagining the energy of your anger being expelled from where it is lodged in your body (running, lifting weights, swimming, riding a bike and many other sports can perform the same service)
> * Hit a cushion or a carpet hanging on the clothesline — again directing the energy outwards
> * Find a sound-proof spot — perhaps your car with windows wound up and stereo on full — and scream and wail from the pit of your stomach
> * Write a letter from the very depths including everything you want to say — no holds barred:

everything that makes you feel angry perhaps in large red Texta colours. Having done that, perhaps over a few sittings, take a match and burn it, imagining the anger you feel inside shrivelling up, fuelling the fire.

Making a life album

Many parents decide to create what has come to be known as a life album for their child. The album is simply the story of your child's life from beginning to end. It will have things like birth and death notices, photographs, foot and handprints (if you have them), a lock of hair, drawings, things the child may have written, your recollections of things they said, stories about them.

A life album contains anything and everything of significance to you that is related to the child. It is an album for you to remember your child by and with which to pay tribute to them.

We made a very simple life album for James about four months after he died, consisting of birth notices, photographs, some drawings by children done for him when he was born and his death notice. It is a very personal thing which we do for ourselves and no-one else.

We often take it out and look at it and sometimes show it to friends. Alice often looks at it. In fact, it is what has helped her to remember her brother so well and make us feel he is still so much a part of the family.

If you decide to make a life album, be prepared for it to be a traumatic process because it will bring back so many memories and feelings. I vividly remember the experience because we started putting it together just after Christmas and I find Christmas much harder than the anniversaries of either his birth or death: it is such a powerful reminder of what could have been. On New Year's Day, we were so tense with each other and on edge. We nearly had a full-scale argument before we realised that sorting through all the photos was renewing the rawness of our grief. So be prepared.

Getting support

There are many groups which offer support to bereaved parents. The best known of these are SANDS, helping parents of stillborn babies or babies that die in-utero; SIDS, working with parents of children who have died as a result of cot death; and Compassionate Friends, a group which works with all bereaved people. While these organisations each have special emphases, they all provide counselling and care for any bereaved person.

If you go to any of them seeking help — and their addresses are at the back of the book — you will find sensitive, loving people who want to do all they can to help you on your journey of grief. Very often these people will themselves have been bereaved. It can be a great comfort to be part of a group of people who have all suffered similar kinds of loss.

You may feel nervous about going along to such a group for the first time, which is a normal reaction. But in our experience it is worth the effort. You discover that other people have been to the brink of despair and lived, that you are not the only one who felt like ending it all, that there is hope for the future.

If you're worried you will have to tell your story the first time you go to such a group, relax. Most group leaders I know are very careful to let you go at your own pace. Besides, if you're asked a question you don't feel like answering, you can always say you're not ready to talk yet. Mostly new members spend the first few meetings just listening to the stories of others. These groups also put you in touch with the latest research in the field which in the case of SIDS and a number of terminal diseases is very helpful.

The other value of such groups is that they can provide us with expert counselling. Depending on the kind of person we are, on how much grief we have already experienced in life and how well — or badly — we have dealt with it, we may well need professional counselling. These groups will have counsellors within them or can direct us to skilled counsellors if needed.

One such counsellor is Sister Brigitte Hirschfield from Brisbane's Mater Hospital. Rosanne and I attended one of Brigitte's grief workshops during the 1988 SIDS Conference and it was enormously healing. We were able to express our grief in drawing and writing and a number of other ways.

Brigitte also works with people individually. She has been especially successful in helping bereaved people to deal with unresolved guilt about the dead person. It is never easy to seek out such counselling help because none of us likes to admit we're not coping. But it is strength, not weakness, to have enough wisdom and humility to admit we need help.

Using faith as a resource

I have no doubt that, were it not for our faith in God, Rosanne and I would no longer be together. Without God, James' death would have blown our relationship to pieces. We have been able to draw on our friendship with Jesus to help keep our marriage together.

I am aware that there are many relationships which, tragically, have not survived the death of a child, even though they also were centred on God. But I cannot speak for those people — I can only speak for myself.

There were many times after James died when we felt we were cracking up mentally. There were times when we felt stretched beyond breaking, when we felt like giving up. What will take away the hurt? Why bother any more? And through it all, it was our faith in Jesus that kept us and held us.

If you have faith, it can be a wonderful resource for you at this time . If you call out to him, he will answer that prayer, however short or anguished.

Much of my praying was done in the form of words written in my journal. It was a very effective way of praying and has been very useful to look back on, to see how I've grown and changed, to see the ways in which God has been at work in my life.

Sometimes bereaved people feel they have no right to ask God to help them if they're not churchgoers. They feel hypocritical. But my experience of God is that he responds to any genuine cry for help whoever it comes from.

God is a God who is always there for people in trouble. Even if you don't go to God in the good times, he won't be offended if you come to him in the bad. Even if you haven't prayed before, you can now. God's door is always open.

7
Moving on

IT IS POSSIBLE TO GRIEVE in both helpful and unhelpful ways. Some grief experts argue that it doesn't matter how you grieve because all grief is helpful. But my experience leads me to believe there are some kinds of grieving that are most unhelpful.

Merry-go-round grief
This kind of grieving stops us from moving on. It can sometimes not only delay our journey of grief, but it can even stop it completely.

Probably the most famous example of this wrong kind of grieving is Miss Havisham in Charles Dickens' *Great Expectations*. Instead of working through her grief about being jilted just before her wedding, Miss Havisham turned her room into a shrine for her shattered hopes and dreams of marriage. She even continued to wear her wedding gown and kept her wedding cake until it became fossilised.

Many parents want to keep their children's clothes and other belongings, which is a very normal reaction. But if we turn our child's room into a shrine for them, perhaps leaving it just as they left it, this will not help us work through our grief. In fact it will be most unhelpful, not only to us, but to the rest of our family. Other family members may well feel that we care more for our dead child than we do for them.

There is a very real danger of putting our dead child on a pedestal. We all do this to a certain extent to the child who has died — we imagine that they were closer to perfection than they really were. In the case of a baby, we may imagine that had they lived they would have been perfect, sleeping through the night at six weeks, doing everything right.

Of course, in time we are likely to come to realise that most of this is not true. But problems can arise if we attribute all the best qualities to the one who has died. We can experience a profound loss of self which can take years to get over.

John Chalmers, in his *Grief Journal*, writes of the way over-dependence can lock us into unhelpful grief:

> One factor that complicates the grieving process is an unhealthy relationship with the person who has died. This may take the form of an over-dependence on the one who died, so that the survivor senses an overwhelming loss of self; or a negative attitude to the one lost, so that the survivor might experience profound guilt in the wake of the loss.
>
> Another factor that complicates grieving is a delay in beginning one's grieving, perhaps by trying to be too strong for others or feeling it is immature to grieve, or because you had to go straight back to

work. A common unhealthy way of avoiding grief is to try to keep the loss buried — with alcohol, over-medication or by filling your life with ceaseless, hectic activity and people.

When our grief isn't allowed healthy expression, it often bursts forth in highly exaggerated reactions at seemingly inappropriate times: being deeply distressed when a pet dies; becoming over-protective; telling others not to go to a funeral or to view the body of the deceased; having to change the subject whenever the name of the dead person is mentioned; becoming deeply distressed over a TV serial or movie.

Sometimes we may even become paralysed by what we see as symptoms of the disease that took our loved one occurring in us.

Another reason we sometimes become locked into prolonging our grief is a wish to stay close to our dead child. We can be tempted to try to pretend it hasn't happened in the hope that somehow that will change things.

Deep down we know this kind of thinking won't change what has happened, but it can be a comfort to cling to in the face of the harshness of reality. If we're not careful we can find ourselves thinking: 'I won't think about all this now because if I don't, it will keep me closer to my child and perhaps if I do it for long enough, it might even bring them back.' But in our heart of hearts we know that nothing can bring them back.

There is also, in those first days, a very real fear of forgetting the appearance of our child. So often I would try to picture James' face in my mind and hold it there. And I would think to myself, 'Even if everyone else forgets you, my darling little son, I never will.' It's important not to allow this very understandable desire to remember our child and everything about them to stop us from going on grieving.

If you see some of these symptoms in yourself, it may mean you have become locked into your grief. This means you will need to spend some time working on getting your grief out into the open. If you feel you're not able to do that, then you will need to seek the help of a professional counsellor. You can find a list of counselling services in the back of the book.

Reorganising your life

I have heard so many bereaved people say something like this: 'This is something I will never get over. There will always be part of me missing.' And every time I hear someone say it I want to say: 'Yes and No. It's true that you will never forget your loved one. They will always have a very special place in your lives and there will always be a sense of loss and a longing that they were still with you. But life moves on. It may never be the same again, but there is hope and there is a future. Things won't seem this black forever.'

I don't say this, however, because I know they are not yet ready to hear it. Grief counsellors agree that it generally takes about eighteen months to two years for life to regain its equilibrium after the death of a loved one, especially if it was unexpected.

Some experts believe it may take up to five years for any real healing to occur after a deep loss. In other words, your life will seem off-balance for at least the first year after the death of your child. It may not take that long. It may take longer. It depends, as always, on the individual.

While there may never come a time in your life when you are able to say, 'All my grief has gone,' the time will probably come when you will feel, 'I've done most of my really deep grieving. I am ready to get on with life now.' You will know when that time comes.

Let's be clear about what we mean by regaining your life balance. Life will never be the same again. It can't be, because the child you had is gone. Acceptance of this is the first step towards some kind of healing. But even then, life cannot be the same as it was before, nor should it be. You are probably a very different person now from the person you were before your child died. Life from now on will be different and it often takes great courage to take the next step towards rebuilding your life without your child.

How do we know when we've reached this point in our grieving? Perhaps it's a little like falling in love. How do you know you're in love? You just know. It is the same with the journey of grief. You just know.

Jenny writes: 'Perhaps it is when you begin to feel the [death] experience is becoming integrated into your life, rather than being a separate or dominating thing. All I know is it is much longer than we expect.'

Joan Blair, who has had two sons die, seventeen-year-old Wayne and ten-year-old Dean, writes:

Christmas again! Each Christmas up till now had been wasted effort. We felt we had to do things simply because it was Christmas. I hadn't enjoyed shopping for Christmas presents for years. I didn't think this one would be much different. I took my little grandson, Trevor, with me.

Something seemed different. For the first time in a long while I noticed the decorations. I wanted to look at them. The resentment was gone. I listened to the carols being played over the public address system. On impulse I picked Trevor up and sang to him. I didn't care who heard me or looked at me. *I felt alive.* It felt so good after so long. It was like being let out into the light after being shut away in the dark. So many things had passed me by. I had not seen or wanted to see. I felt now, 'I want something to look forward to. I want to live!'

It may be a generalisation, but I believe it is true to say that when you are more concerned about the present and the future than you are about the past, it is a sign that you are beginning to regain your life-balance.

There are some concrete things you can do to help yourself reorganise your life. One of them is to read books like this one. Read whatever material you can get hold of from SIDS, SANDS, Compassionate Friends or any other organisation that helps bereaved people. Read other books by bereaved parents, some of which are listed in the back.

Become part of a support group where you can share with others who have been through similar experiences. Start a journal or diary where you can write down how you're feeling and can record your progress on this journey.

Another helpful thing to do is to indulge yourself

more often than you would normally. Book in for the occasional massage, which is wonderfully therapeutic. Go out for dinner or book into a hotel for a weekend.

You may be thinking, 'We can't afford these sorts of luxuries. They're too expensive!' But more than any other time in your life, you need to have a bit of luxury and do some enjoyable things you've never done before. Life can be so terribly serious, coping with all these heavy emotions and traumas; it is crucial that you make time to play.

Another important area is that of diet. Grief can lower our resistance to infection. Often our immune system can be impaired and we can lack the antibodies we would normally have to fight off infections. So we need to eat as little processed food as possible and eat as much fresh fruit and vegetables as we are able to — where possible we should eat them raw. We should make sure we have enough fibre in our diet, which shouldn't be too difficult with the variety of brans now available to us.

We may even need, for a time, to take a course of vitamin tablets — though a doctor or naturopath should be consulted to make sure we really need them.

It is also very important to get enough sleep. However, often it is this very area that is most disrupted in bereaved people. We can have trouble going to sleep or find ourselves waking up at three o'clock in the morning with our minds racing. I have found that a long warm bath can be a wonderful aid to relaxation and sleep. We're such busy people that we sometimes forget that it is still possible to take a bath. If you do wake up at 3.00 a.m. and can't get back to sleep, don't lie there and toss and turn. Get up and do something. Make yourself a milk drink or do some writing or watch television.

Exercise is another important prerequisite for sleep. Many of us are so desk-bound that we don't get the exercise we need and this can affect our sleeping patterns. We need, so the experts tell us, three twenty minute periods of intense exercise every week. It can be running along a beach, power-walking, riding a bike, or simply walking briskly.

The other great advantage of exercise is that it gets you out of the house, which is especially important for mothers. There is nothing that will drive a person to the brink more quickly than being stuck in a home twenty-four hours a day with only children to talk to and pick up after.

I have also discovered that simple relaxation exercises, stretching and quiet deep breathing are a great help. Many people find that meditation is very renewing. However, you may find remaining still and quiet very difficult in the early days of your grief. Don't expect too much of yourself despite what some books may recommend as the thing to do.

Another very positive way to help reorganise your life may be to set yourself a task. Some parents decide they want to do something to help other children who have the same disease their child died of or who died in the same way their child died.

This book grew out of my desire to 'do something' for James, but it's also done a great deal for me. My hope and prayer is that it has also done something for others.

May God bless you as you continue on your journey of grief. Knowing that this journey will one day end is what keeps me going — knowing that the time will come, in the words of Julian of Norwich, 'when all things shall be well and all manner of things shall be well'.

Appendix I:
About cot death

SIDS stands for Sudden Infant Death Syndrome — the sudden, unexpected and unexplained death of babies in the first two years of life. The majority of cot deaths occur between two and six months.

SIDS is not a new phenomenon. Most cases of 'smothering' or 'overlaying' are almost certainly SIDS. The first recorded instance of SIDS can be found in 1 Kings chapter 3, verses 16 to 28 in the Old Testament.

Cot death is known as SIDS because there is not just one factor that causes the baby to die. It is a syndrome. There may be forty or fifty factors that contribute to the death of children.

Some of these are identifiable: extremes of temperature, smoking by the mother during pregnancy and passively by the child after it has been born, prematurity, low birth weight, being male (about sixty per cent of cot deaths are male) and viral infection just prior to death and bottle feeding (breast-fed babies are at less risk).

Forty per cent of babies which die in cot deaths have some kind of viral infection. The infection is usually mild and did not cause their death, but it appears to have contributed to it.

The most dramatic finding in recent years in Australia has been research that shows a significant decrease in infant deaths when babies sleep on their sides or backs instead of their stomachs. The Menzies Research Centre (for population health) in Hobart has monitored a fifty-eight per cent decrease in the number of cot deaths in Tasmania during the past twelve months due at least, in part, to the change in sleeping position.

Parents of children who exhibit a number of these SIDS factors are advised that their child may be at risk and that they should consider using a cot monitor. Cot monitors are now quite sophisticated and monitor the baby's breathing, not just movement. However, there is little point in parents putting their baby on a cot monitor unless they are proficient in CPR (Cardio Pulmonary Resuscitation) and are willing to use it if necessary.

There is also concern among health care professionals that some parents believe cot monitors will prevent their baby from dying. All the monitor will do is to alarm if the child stops breathing. The hard reality is that even then there is no guarantee of saving the child. I have heard of parents having their child stop breathing while they were holding them, but of not being able to save them. It seems that in some cases while it is possible to start the baby breathing again, they will still die.

There is still not agreement among researchers and doctors as to the exact nature of SIDS. If there was we would probably know how to stop it. Some believe that SIDS is extended apnoea, where the brain forgets to tell the lungs to breath. If the child is found within a few minutes of having stopped breathing, such measures as being shaken or picked up or even the noise of a cot monitor alarm can often reactivate breathing.

However, all I have read and heard causes me to believe that SIDS is not just infantile apnoea. If it were, we would be able to save all babies who were found within a minute or so of stopping breathing. This is very much a layman's point of view, but I believe that, whatever SIDS is, it is something that switches off the respiratory system and at times nothing we do seems to be able to switch it back on.

Despite millions of dollars of research into SIDS and the wonderful public response in Australia to Red Nose Day, we seem to be little closer to discovering a way of stopping this terrible thing that causes more deaths than anything else in this age group.

Appendix II:
Helpful resources

Grief support groups in Australia

Compassionate Friends Inc., Bereaved Parents' Support and Information Centre, Suite 3, Rear 205 Blackburn Rd, Syndal, Victoria 3149, phone: (03) 232 8222

Stillbirth and Neonatal Death Support (SANDS). The State branches of SANDS are usually listed in the phone directory. The address of SANDS National Council is c/- PO Box 493, Lane Cove, NSW 2066.

Sudden Infant Death Syndrome (SIDS), National SIDS Council Of Australia, 1227 Malvern Rd, Malvern, Victoria 3144, phone: (03) 822 0766

National Association Of Loss And Grief (NALAG). There are branches of this group throughout Australia. NALAG often holds seminars on coping with grief and is a very useful contact.

These four groups all have a wide range of books, booklets and tapes on grief as well as counselling services.

Grief support groups in the United Kingdom
National Association of Bereavement Services, 68 Chalton Street, London, NW1 1JR, phone: 071 247 1080 (24 hour) and 071 247 0617 (administration)

CRUSE, Cruse House, 126 Sheen Rad, Richmond, Surrey, TW9 1UR, phone: 081 940 4818

The Society of Compassionate Friends, 6 Denmark Street, Bristol, BS1 5DQ, phone: 0272 292778

Foundation for the Study of Infant Deaths (Cot Death Research & Support), 35 Belgrave Square, London, SW1X 8QB, phone: 071 235 1721.
Contact: Erica De'Ath

Stillbirth and Neo-natal Death Society (SANDS), 28 Portland Place, London 1N 4DE, phone: 071 436 588
Contact: Roma Iskander

Books for adults
A Death in the Family, Jean Richardson, Lion, 1992
A Grief Observed, C.S.Lewis, Faber and Faber, 1961. A husband's response to the death of his wife. A brutally honest look at raw grief which doesn't pretend to have the answers.
Coming to New Life, John Chalmers, the Liturgical Commission of the Roman Catholic Church in Australia, PO Box 282, GPO Brisbane 4000,

Australia. Highly recommended for journal-writing as outlined in chapter 6.

Coping with Grief, Mal McKissock, ABC Enterprises, 1985. One of the best small books available on grief.

Cot Deaths, Jacquelyn Luben, Thomasons Publishing Group, 1986

Explaining Death to Children, Earl Grollman (ed.), Beacon Press, 1969

Good Grief, Granger E. Westberg, Fortress, 1962

Healing Grief, Amy Hillyard Jensen, Medic Publishing Co, 1980

Helping Children Understand Death, William D. Nelson, Tobin Brothers, 1973. A short booklet, but very useful in helping grieving children. Often available from funeral parlours.

Losing A Child, Elaine Storkey, Lion, 1989

On Death and Dying, Elisabeth Kubler-Ross, MacMillan, 1969

Shadow of Loss: A Mother Remembers, Joan Enid Blair, Available from Joan Blair, c/- PO Kiama, NSW 2533, Australia. A moving account of a mother's grief, following the tragic death of two sons.

The Anatomy of Bereavement, Beverley Raphael, Basic Books Inc, 1983. Beverley Raphael is Professor of Psychiatry at the University of Queensland. Her book is a scholarly analysis of the grieving process. It isn't light reading, but is full of insight and wisdom. Well worth taking the time to read.

The Bereaved Parent, Harriet Sannoff Schiff, Crown Publishers, 1977

The Problem of Pain, C. S. Lewis, Fontana, 1965

The Ways of a Philosophical Scrivener, Martin Gardner, The Harvester Press, 1983. Especially chapters 15 and 16 on evil. An expensive book. Get it from the library.
When a Baby Suddenly Dies, Janet Deveson Lord, Hill of Content, 1987. An excellent book on Sudden Infant Death Syndrome.
When Bad Things Happen to Good People, Harold Kushner, Shocken, 1981
When the Dream is Shattered, Judith and Michael Murray, Lutheran Publishing House, Adelaide, 1988. Written from the perspective of psychologist parents who have lost three children as the result of miscarriage and neonatal death.
Your Healing Is Within You, Jim Glennon, Hodder and Stoughton, 1978. A wonderfully helpful book on healing and wholeness.

Books for children/teenagers
Emma Says Goodbye, Carolyn Nistrom, Lion, 1990. On the death of an aunty.
Grandpa and Me, Marlee and Benny Alex, Lion, 1981. On the death of a grandpa.
Kirsty's Kite, Carol Curtis Stilz and Gwen Harrison, Albatross, 1988. On the death of a mother.
Losing Someone You Love: When a Brother or Sister Dies, Elizabeth Richter, G.P. Dutnam & Sons, 1986. For teenagers.
What Happened When Grandma Died, Peggy Barker, Lutheran Publishing House, 1984

Videos, Australia
Understanding the Concept of Death (mixed media

kit). Available from Lady Gowrie Child Centre, Hobart, Tasmania 1990. Kit consists of two videos, five books, workshop notes, *Today's Child* articles, reading lists. Contact the Lady Gowrie Health Centre in any State of Australia.

Helping Children Understand Death, Lady Gowrie Child Centre, Hobart, Tasmania 1984, twelve minutes. Interview with a psychologist aimed at helping children cope with death. Contact the Lady Gowrie Health Centre in any State of Australia.

Interview with the author and his wife about the death of their son. Originally shown on Network Ten News in 1989 and now available courtesy of Network Ten, Australia. The interview goes for just over twenty minutes and we are happy to send you a copy at cost (A$15). Write to us at The Rectory, Franklin Street, Triabunna, Tasmania 7190. Overseas readers need to add A$10 and pay by bank draft in Australian dollars.

Most large funeral parlours also have videos, books and booklets that are available to bereaved people.

Feature films

There are also a number of feature films which deal very well with the issues of grief. The best I've seen are *Shadowlands*, the moving story of C.S. Lewis' wife Joy, who died of cancer, and *Steel Magnolias*, which handles sensitively the grief of coping with the death of an adult child. Look out for them on video.

Case histories mentioned have been altered in location, sex and circumstances, in an effort to maintain confidentiality, except where permission has been given to use real names.